the PEACOCK

MANIFESTO

First published in 2001 by I.M.P. FICTION

I.M.P. Fiction Ltd
P. O. Box 14691, London, SE1 2ZA
Fax: 020 7357 8608   E-mail: info@impbooks.com

This Edition © I.M.P. Fiction 2001
A catalogue record for this book is available
from The British Library

ISBN 0-9533275-5-8
1 2 3 4 5 6 7 8 9 10

Printed and bound in Great Britain.

Cover Photography: Karn David
Cover Designed by Karn David, Phil Gambrill and I.M.P. Fiction.
Visit Peacock Johnson at: www.peacock-johnson.com
Visit I.M.P. FICTION at: www.impbooks.com

The Peacock Manifesto

by
Stuart David

I.M.P. Fiction
London

PROLOGUE

They call me Peacock.

Why?

The tattoo. I wear it on my shoulder. I had it done in my teens, in admiration of the bird. I still admire the bird today. I admire the way it looks. I admire the way it struts. I admire the way it preens.

And did it hurt?

Did it fuck.

But perhaps even without the tattoo they would still call me Peacock. I like to strut. I like to preen. I keep myself colourful. I wear a white vest to give the tattoo as much exposure as possible, but when it gets cooler I like to wear a good Hawaiian shirt on top. A good vintage one. None of this modern shite.

I keep my hair slicked back and my long moustache well trimmed. I like a good pair of vintage trousers too. I like to look good. There's no point in slinking about in the shadows like a cunt. That never got anybody anywhere, and I'm certainly going somewhere.

You'll see.

Right now I'm on my way to Chicago. Sitting high above the clouds in the sunshine. There's a start already. When I left Glasgow this morning the rain was pissing down. Bucketing. But here I am now with my head up high above the clouds.

Fucking magic.

I've got an idea, you see - and I'm taking that to Chicago. I'm on my way to meet a guy who can turn ideas into something real. A friend of a friend of a friend. I took the risk of telling a guy I know that I had the idea, and he said he might know someone who could help. Someone who could make it real. I'm strictly an ideas man, but then again - that's the most important part, eh? I just hope this guy can do what I've been told he can do. He fucking better be able to. I spent just about the last money I had on this fucking flight.

There's an idiot sitting next to me. But when's there not, eh? This one's in a suit. As soon as we were up and it started to get stuffy I pulled off the Hawaiian shirt and he clocked the tattoo.

"That's a fine piece of work," he told me.

So I let him know that he should keep his eyes off it, keep his eyes off me, and forget about trying to make any more conversation.

He thought the bird was a fucking budgie.

Fucking tool.

But there's not been another peep out of him since then. The prick's been pretending to sleep since my wee warning. I can see him slightly opening his eyes and risking a worried glance at me every now and again, and then he makes a fucked-up noise to try and convince me he's asleep for sure. But he's stopped bothering me now, and as long as I know he won't try and talk to me again I'm happy. And I've got my idea to keep me occupied.

I'll tell you what I feel like up here - carrying this thing. I feel a bit like my Uncle Tam. Or how I imagine he must have felt, the day he fucked himself up for good. While he was making his journey at least.

He was eighty-two years old then, and the poor cunt had been impotent for over twenty years. But on this particular morning he woke up with one of the most impressive hard-ons he'd ever had. Hard as a rock, he said. So - still half asleep - he rolled over towards his wife, and she wasn't there. He started shouting on her, and as he woke up more he remembered she'd gone to stay at her sister's. Typical, eh? So he thought about working it off himself, but he decided that would be a waste. And instead he got out of bed, half expecting the thing to fall away as soon as he stood up. But it stayed. He could hardly fucking believe it.

He got himself dressed, carefully - then he went downstairs and it was still the same. He said there was something almost supernatural about it; as if he was an adolescent again. And he got outside and got on the bus, and of course that could only help. He'd expected it might go down once he got amongst people, out of a sense of decency; but not at all. It stayed. And he had to cover it with his *hat*.

So he travelled like that all the way to his wife's sister's, early in the morning, on a bus full of people going to work.

When he got to the house everything was still quiet there. He knew he was taking his chances if he knocked the door and had to talk to his wife's sister first. He'd have to think up a reason for why he was there and then risk his wife coming downstairs to sit and drink tea with them. So instead the old fool went round to the back of the house and started climbing up the fucking drainpipe to the spare room. And he got pretty close too. He got close enough to knock on the window, and close enough that his wife came and opened the curtains. And he managed to hold on. He managed to hold on while she looked scared then just confused. And he managed to hold on while she opened the window. But then, as a way of explaining his strange visit, the old idiot took one hand off the drainpipe to point at his dick bulging in his trousers, and he fell all the way onto the path beneath them.

Never walked again, and he certainly never got another

9

hard-on.

But at that one point, that moment in the day when he was travelling on the bus with his hat covering his prick - he must have felt pretty much how I feel just now, up here above these clouds. And I only have to hope this Yank cunt I'm on my way to see comes through for me. And I don't end up lying in the garden like Uncle Tam.

PART I

I

Idiot-boy in the next seat kept his eyes closed all the way down. He pretended to be sleeping as we started to descend, and even after we landed. Right on through the plane moving into park, and then stopping.

No one can sleep through a landing. I was shitting myself. And I'll bet if Tam had had to fly to his wife's sister's the landing would have assured he was still walking right up till the day he died.

But this fool pretended to sleep right through it.

"Please stay in your seats while the 'Fasten Seat-belts' sign remains lit," they said. And he pretended to be sleeping through that. Then, as soon as it beeped and the light went out, he was up like a shot and pushing to get off the plane.

"Aye, run," I shouted at him, and a lot of other people turned round, but he didn't turn round. I didn't see him again. I didn't see him at the bit where you get your bags, or outside the building.

Wanker.

I got a taxi outside. The cunt who was driving had no idea what I was saying.

"What? Where you wanna go?"

Over and over.

I had to write it down and show it to him.

Fucking Yanks.

Some of what we passed through looked pretty rough. Plenty in Glasgow looks pretty rough, but mostly cause it's fucked-up. Either someone's fucked it up or there's no money to fix it. Some of this looked like it had been *built* like that. Bars on the windows and doors. Fucking mad.

It was fucking freezing in the back of the taxi. The cunt had the windows down and he gave me the "What?" treatment again.

"Put the window up, pal."

"What?"

"It's fucking freezing."

"What?"

"Ah, fuck off."

I said that quieter than the rest, but the prick understood *that*. He stopped.

"Get out," he said.

So I tried it myself.

"What?"

"Get out my cab."

I looked out the window.

"Get out."

"Calm down, pal," I told him, and kept looking out my window. "Let's get going."

Then I heard something hitting against the glass that was between him and me and I looked up.

The cunt had a gun.

"Get out," he said again. So I grabbed my bag and got out. And there I was amongst those buildings with the bars on the windows and doors.

I got another taxi pretty quickly. I don't think the guy was going to stop but I didn't give him any fucking choice. I got right out into the road and stood in front of him. Then I jumped in the back while he was still shouting. I showed him the bit of paper I showed the first guy and just smiled. Pretended I didn't

12

speak the fucking language. It was fucking easier. That calmed him down too, thinking I was just some daft foreign bastard.

It didn't stop him talking though. He talked all the way from there to the hotel, about how crazy a place America is, and exactly what I'd think of it. What I'd like, what I wouldn't. What I'd do and what would happen to me. I shrugged now and again to try and convince him I didn't understand a word. He didn't seem to have the brains to realise that if I couldn't speak English I probably wouldn't understand what the fuck he was talking about either. Or maybe he just didn't care.

Still, I made it here. I found it pretty confusing that I'd been travelling for fifteen hours, and it was only nine hours since I'd left the house, by my watch. If I'd been at home it would have been getting on for night-time, but it was only the afternoon. I couldn't get my head round that. I felt like going to bed, but you can't go to bed in the afternoon. So I went downstairs to the bar.

★

I had a day to wait until my guy was due to arrive. He wasn't coming till the next afternoon. Coming in from New York. Apparently he knew somewhere we could work cheaply in Chicago – so that's why I was there. I hoped the cunt would turn up. My mate who spoke to his mate likes to think he's such a big fucking mover that he put the whole thing together himself. He thought that would impress me. It fucking impressed him.

"Maybe I should speak to the guy first," I kept saying to him.

"No need," he would tell me. "It's all taken care of, Peacock. Just remember, I'm on twenty per cent if it all works out."

Tit.

I should have fucking spoke to him though. Just to sort it out.

I know a few things about the guy. I know he's not long out of the jail. And I know he's gotten into this new thing now. I know he can take the ideas and make them real. I think he's

13

realised the same thing as me, that this is where the money's to be made now. There's nothing wrong with a bit of crime on the side, to keep you going, but no one makes the big money there anymore. It's all moved out into other places. A lot of it has moved into talking about crime. In the films and that. And a lot of it has moved into this thing we're about to get involved in.

As soon as I arrived at my hotel I opened my bag, and unwrapped my wee portable CD player from the towels that were protecting it. And then I went into the pocket of the bag. I felt that thrill again as I pulled the CD out of there. The same thrill I got when the idea first occurred to me. That Uncle Tam feeling. And I slapped it into the CD player and listened again.

Each time I go to listen to it again I shit myself in case it doesn't still hold up. But it always does. It's perfect. It's a stroke of fucking genius. And as soon as we get a dance beat onto this, and some of those fucking techno noises – some of that fucking scratching – it's going to sell a million. Two million. Ten fucking million.

If this guy comes through and knows his stuff it'll be a fucking worldwide hit. I don't have the fucking first iota about how any of that stuff gets done, but that's not the important part. The important part is the idea – and *what* a fucking idea.

Wait till you hear it.

Wait till you hear what we're going to make a dance record from. Are you ready?

Glen Campbell. Rhinestone-fucking-Cowboy.

Eh?

Ha ha....

II

When I came back up from the bar I phoned the wife, but I still hadn't got my head round the time change.

"What's wrong, Peacock?"

"Nothing."

"*Nothing*? What the fuck are you phoning me for then?"

"Eh?"

"What *time* is it, Peacock?"

"Ten o'clock."

"Not here. Not here it's not. It's four o'clock in the morning here, Peacock. Phone me tomorrow afternoon, you big moron."

And then she hung up.

Charming, eh? What a wee smasher. Six thousand miles I'd travelled and she didn't even ask me how the fucking trip was. She was awake by then anyway; it wouldn't have killed her. But she's still in the huff, you see. She's in the huff cause I never brought her with me. I kept telling her I was coming here to work, not for a holiday. But all she kept saying was, "What the fuck do you know about music? You big baboon."

I told her.

"I don't know a fucking thing about it, but I know a good idea."

And that always shut her up. She knows it's a good idea too.

I got a good sleep after I'd phoned her, though. Just knowing it was four in the morning at home put me out like a light. I didn't wake up till the phone woke me, and I'd no idea where I was.

"Mr Johnson?"

"Eh?"

"Guest for you, sir?"

"What? Who the fuck's this?"

"This is front desk, sir. We have a guest for you? Shall I send him up?"

I looked at the clock then. Fucking two o'clock in the afternoon.

"Tell him to wait," I said. "I'll come down."

I took my time. I had a shower. I fixed myself up. When I got downstairs he was the only person in the lobby. He looked pretty ridiculous. For a start the cunt was wearing a hairnet. A *hairnet*. Like my fucking granny used to wear to keep her rollers in place. I liked his boots though. Snakeskin they looked like.

He stood up when he saw me.

"Peacock?" he said.

"That's me, son," I told him, and he reached out his hand.

"Glad to meet you," he said, and then he introduced himself. Are you ready for this? Just keep in mind that he said it with a straight face.

He said, "I'm Evil Bob."

Can you believe it?

There was no way I could keep a straight face.

"You're fucking joking," I said.

But he held up his knuckles. It was tattooed there.

He didn't find it amusing that I'd found it amusing.

"So why do they call you Peacock?" he asked, and I showed him the bird.

"Looks more like a parrot," he said. "Or a cockatiel."

We stared at each other for a bit, then he laughed. Then I laughed. It seemed okay. So we went out to a sandwich shop further up the street, to talk some business.

"What the fuck is that?" I asked him when he brought our sandwiches to the table.

"What?"

"That."

"Ham and cheese. You asked for ham and cheese."

"Not that much ham. Not that much cheese. That's a whole fucking packet of both, pal."

"Welcome to America," he said.

I stripped some of it off. Fuck that.

"So," Bob said, as he sat down, "you're the guy."

I assured him that I was.

"Well," he said, "let's hope this works out."

And then he started eating his own thing. Full to bursting with vegetables and what looked like grass.

He was quite a skinny wee guy, but he could eat. He didn't strip a single vegetable off, and his speed amazed me. He didn't look up or say a word till he'd finished, and even though I'd knocked mine down to a normal size before I started I was only halfway through the first slice by the time he was done.

"That's better," he said. Then he started on his coffee.

"Well, from what I've heard it seems we'll make a great team," he said.

"Should do, son. Should do."

"Did they tell you what I've got?"

"Not a word. They only told me you were the guy."

"That's pretty much all they told me about you. But I think you'll be impressed. I think we're onto something."

He dragged his bag up onto the table and I laughed at the logo on it. Bolsov Ballet.

"Quite the faggot, eh?" he said. "I used to dance there."

"Dance?"

"Modern dance. Then someone knocked me off my bike. Broke both my legs."

"Probably for the best," I told him.

"Forget that," he said. "This is the shit."

He pulled a pair of headphones out of the bag, and put his hands back inside.

"Put those on," he said, so I did. A Stones song came on. Fucking Jagger whooping away. Then it stopped.

"What do you think?" he asked.

"Eh?"

He nodded at me and winked.

"What?" I asked him, and he looked a bit hurt.

"You don't like it?"

"It sounds okay."

"So you think you can do something with it?"

"What?"

"We just need to repeat that one part. It'll fly. As soon as you've added some beats and maybe a house piano it'll be fantastic.

It can't fail."

I looked down at all the spare meat and cheese on my plate. "Ah, fuck..." I said.

III

I'd got the time difference worked out by the next time I phoned the wife, but I didn't tell her about what had happened. She'd have gone mental. I just told her that I'd met the guy, and he seemed like an okay guy. I didn't tell her he'd been expecting me to do the same job I'd been expecting him to do. And I didn't tell her I'd lost the head with him a bit, there in the sandwich shop.

I can't remember all what I shouted in there now, but I think I scared the wee guy. Some of it was directed at him, but most of it was about that cunt who'd sent me over there in the first place. I remember I started throwing bits of meat at the window at one point, and he just sat there staring at me. And then, when I'd settled down again, he asked me what my idea had been.

"Ach... It doesn't matter, son," I told him.

"I'm interested," he said. "Mine was good enough to bring me in from New York. I'm interested in what brought you all the way from Scotland?"

I shook my head. "Forget it, pal," I told him.

"Come on, Peacock," he said. "What was the song? Tell me the song."

I stood up. "For fuck sake," I said. "Okay. Come and I'll let you hear it."

So we went back to the hotel, and I dug out the CD player. I gave him the headphones and when he'd put them on I sparked it up.

I watched his face.

I could hear the song playing faintly while he listened, but his expression didn't change. Then, after about a verse had passed he took the headphones off.

"How do I stop this, Peacock?" he asked, and I showed him the button. He pressed it. Then the cunt stood up and shook my fucking hand.

"Peacock," he said. "You've done it, man. That's... it's genius."

"Fuck off," I said.

"I'm serious, man. This is something. Glen *Campbell* – Jesus Christ! We've *got* to get this made, Peacock. We have to. How fucking hard can it be?"

"Pretty fucking hard, apparently."

"Bullshit. We'll..."

He started scrambling about the room then. Opening drawers, closing them again. Looking in the cupboards.

"What the fuck are you looking for?" I asked him. "Get out of my fucking stuff, Bob."

But he kept going till he had what he wanted.

"Here we are," he said, and he sat down on the bed with a copy of the yellow pages. He leafed through it and then tore a page out.

"This is all we need, Peacock," he said. "This is our fucking ticket to success. Are you ready?"

"Ready for what?" I asked him.

"Ready to go out," he said. "Come on, there's a few things we need."

I didn't tell the wife about where we ended up either. And I particularly didn't tell her what happened once we got there. That would have driven her totally fucking up the wall. Where we ended up was in a music shop – and, right enough – that might not have bothered her too much. But what happened once we got in there was this: I spent another four hundred fucking dollars.

And, believe me, that wouldn't have made her too fucking happy, I can tell you.

"Okay, man," Bob had said to the guy behind the counter. "We're looking to make a dance record. Tell us what we need."

And the guy had started talking. And talking. And Bob, the

wee prick, he nodded and frowned as if he knew what was going on, as if he understood every fucking word. And the guy had kept at it, and Bob had nodded and frowned some more - until it had happened. Suddenly we'd bought this fucking... *machine*.

Eight hundred dollars between us.

"This is fucking madness," I said to Bob as we carried it back to the hotel room, but the wee man was fucking convinced. He was going to make a worldwide dance hit on this thing.

"You heard the guy," he told me. "This is what they all use, Peacock. It's going to happen."

So we unpacked it, and we turned it on. Then we just fucking stood there.

Bob was grinning from ear to ear, practically *skipping*. He was rubbing his hands together and chuckling away, but I was just staring at it. It was a grey box covered in pads and nobs, with a screen up in the corner.

"Now what?" I asked him.

"Now this," he said, and he picked up the manual. He took a quick flip through it and then handed it to me.

"How much of this is in English?" I asked him, and I looked towards the back - hoping for it to turn into French or Japanese after the first few pages. But it didn't. The whole fucking thing was in English, all three hundred-odd pages of it. And there were all these fucking scientific diagrams and charts.

"Listen, wee man," I told him, and gave the book back to him. "You come and get me when you've worked this thing out. Until then, I'll be in the bar."

But I had to give him his due. I was only on my third pint when he came down to get me. And the cunt was still fucking smiling.

He looks like someone when he smiles. Someone from the films. I've been trying to work out who it is, but I can't get a hold of it. I will though - I'll work it out. And I'll let you know when I do.

"How did it go?" I asked him as he sat down.

"Sweet, Peacock," he said. "I've got it going. It's easy. Come on up and we'll try something."

"Let me finish my drink first, son," I told him. "Do you want one?"

He shook his head. He was fucking itching to get back up there again, you could tell. So I drank mine down quickly and then we went up.

The thing looked just as baffling to me as it had done before, but Bob set about hooking up my CD player to it, and then he pushed a few buttons. He started the CD and pushed a few more, and I heard the song faint again in the headphones. Then it stopped.

"Alright," Bob said, "Put these on." And he gave me the headphones. "Ready?" he asked, still with that grin, and I almost got a grip on who he looked like, but it slipped away.

He held one finger up in the air, above a button on the machine, and in an exaggerated way he let it fall down onto the button. Then the song started to play, from the machine, and Bob was rubbing his hands again.

"How about *that*, Peacock?" he asked me. "How *about* that?"

"Aye, it's a start, son," I said.

"Ah, but watch this," he told me, and he pushed a few more buttons. Then he got himself confused and the grin disappeared.

"Fuck..." he said. "How did...?"

He leafed rapidly through the manual, and came back to the machine. Again the exaggerated finger above the button.

"Ready?"

I shrugged, and down it came. The song started, and when it got to the end of the bit he'd recorded it repeated again. And again. It wasn't too smooth, but Bob was up on his feet, skipping about.

"Alright!" he shouted. "All-fucking-right!"

He dug into the Boston Ballet bag and pulled out a quarter bottle of whisky, and he went into the toilet and came back with the plastic cups for rinsing your teeth.

"Let's get to work," he said.

"Aye, son," I told him. "I'll get to work on the whisky, and you get on with the tune."

As it turned out, though, I pitched in with him pretty quickly. The whisky got me excited, and I could hear what he was doing coming through the headphones. We'd got a CD of drum beats free with the machine, and he'd loaded all those in and he was hitting away at them.

After about five minutes I found myself pulling the headphones off him and wading right in there myself. It was easy. It was a breeze, this music thing. And it was good fucking fun too.

"Record this, Bob," I told him, when I'd worked a bit out. And somehow he knew how to do it. Then he had a shot again.

We kept on like that for hours. One of us drinking while the other one worked. Then we'd swap.

We sent down to the bar for a few more bottles, and we were pretty fucked-up by the time we'd finished.

I didn't tell the wife about that.

I phoned her just after we'd woken up the next morning. My head was fucking pounding. Bob had slept on the floor, and he was being sick in the bathroom when I phoned her. Sorry - the fucking *rest* room. He was being sick in the fucking rest room. I didn't tell her that either. And here's one more thing I didn't tell her: I didn't tell her how excitedly we'd got up to listen to what we did the night before, despite the hangovers.

"Turn it on, Bob," I'd shouted at him, as he'd fumbled with the buttons. "Come on, let's fucking go."

And on the lights came.

He put the headphones on, but I pulled them off of him.

"Spark it up, son," I told him, and it started. And I listened. And I looked at him. And it sounded *shite*. Absolutely *shite*.

I passed the headphones to him and I shook my head. He put them on. He took them off. Then he ran off to the "rest room" to be sick.

I'll tell you what it sounded like. One night, the guy upstairs from us went metal. He started smashing things up there; throwing stuff at the walls, and smashing things on the floor. I had Glen on the stereo at the time. And that's exactly how the thing we'd made sounded. Fucking chaos. Just all this clattering and banging while this one bit of the song we'd recorded played over and over, and stuttered and skipped at the bit where it repeated, like it was a record jumping and stuck.

It was awful. Fucking Jesus awful.

"We're going to make a million," I told the wife. "Ten million. I'll phone you tomorrow, hen." And I hung up.

The wee man staggered back into the room.

"Bob," I said. "We don't know the first fucking thing about this. We're fucked."

He sat down on the corner of the bed, rubbing his head.

"The idea though..." he said. "Let me make one phonecall, Peacock. Maybe my guy knows another guy. There must be a way."

Then he got up and, quite methodically, he started packing the machine back into the box. Replacing all the polystyrene chunks and stuff. And when he was done he looked around the room.

"Fuck," he shouted. "FUCK!!"

IV

It wasn't a friendly thing I did, but it had to be done.

I pushed the wee man up against the wall, and lifted him up off the floor – just a couple of inches. I had one hand on his throat, but that wasn't how I held him up. I didn't want to kill the wee bastard. My other hand was on his belt, and I held him up by that. The hand on his throat was just to steady him.

Still, I gave it a wee squeeze all the same – just to keep him scared.

"Do you understand me, son?" I shouted, loud, leaning in close to his face. "Do you fucking understand what I'm talking about?"

He had his eyes closed, but he nodded.

"Cause I'll fucking kill you," I whispered. "If you disappear and I find out someone else has made this record, I'll fucking find you."

I let him down then, but I kept him up against the wall. He opened his eyes.

"Do you understand me?" I asked him again.

"I understand, Peacock," he said. "I understand. Fucking *hell*."

So I let him go and I shook his hand.

"Just as long as it's clear," I told him.

"It's clear," he said. "It's fucking clear."

"Alright. Alright, wee man. Go and straighten yourself up and we'll take this thing back to the shop."

He'd made a phone call just before that, from the room. He'd phoned his guy, and it turned out his guy knew a producer out on the West Coast; someone with a studio who he thought would be able to do the job we were looking for. Apparently the producer owed Bob's guy a favour, so he said he'd fix it up and we were back in action again.

We hatched a plan to take the machine back to the shop and use the money to hire a car - and Bob said he'd drive us out there. I knew I was stuck with him then. I don't have a licence, and without his contacts I was fucked. I didn't know a soul in the whole fucking country. So we made an agreement - if we managed to get the thing made we'd split everything fifty-fifty. And all that was left for me to do then was give him that wee warning. I could picture myself waking up one morning in some motel, and the fucker would be gone. Off to the West Coast with my idea and there would be fuck-all I could do about it. So I had to make things clear to him. It wasn't a friendly thing to do, and I'm getting to quite like him. But it had to be done.

Just so's he knows.

★

We had quite a carry on at the music shop, trying to get the money back on the machine. For a start I'd lost the receipt.

"Come on, man," Bob said to the guy. "You remember us, don't shit me."

"I remember you," the guy said. "But I need a receipt."

Then he wanted to know why we didn't like it.

"This is our most popular sampler," he told us. "We've never had any complaints about this machine before."

"Oh, it's a good machine," Bob said. "It's not the machine we have a problem with. It's us. The machine's fine, but I'll let you in on a secret." He lowered his voice. "We *stink*," he said. "We tried, but... you would have died if you'd heard what we came up with. Tell him about it, Peacock."

"It sounded like someone killing themselves," I said.

"What?"

"It was a fiasco."

"What?"

"Ah, fuck off..." Under my breath again. And again the cunt understood it perfectly.

"Get out," he shouted. "I don't need this shit, guys. Get out of here."

"Okay, okay..." Bob said. "Peacock..." He put his hand on my back. "Wait outside, man. Wait outside."

"I'm sorry," he said to the guy. "He didn't mean that. He gets... frustrated. Let's see if we can sort this out."

I went outside, shaking my head. Yanks and their fucking guns. I had a feeling that's what was coming next – just like the guy in the fucking taxi. So I went outside.

Bob came out about ten minutes later, waving the money.

"We're set, Peacock," he said.

"What did you tell him?" I asked.

"I told him a few stories. Just a few stories."

So we went and got the car. Bob took the hairnet off for that and smoothed his hair down, then he left me outside with his jacket.

I couldn't believe it when he drove back out. I couldn't believe what he drove back out in.

"What the fuck is that?" I shouted as he stopped and rolled the window down.

"This is class," he shouted back. "Get in."

It was quite a car. Some kind of green sports car. I sank into the passenger seat. He pulled away and it hardly made a noise.

"How about this?" he asked. "I told them to give me something compact. I told them to give me something budget. This is what I got."

"It's fucking comfortable," I said.

"I needs to be. We're going a long way."

Back at the hotel I phoned the wife again, to tell her we were moving on. And since the wee man was out of earshot, taking the bags down to the car, I told her about having him up against the wall. That gave her a laugh. I told her his hairnet had slipped off and that cracked her up. I thought I'd told her about his hairnet before, but I hadn't. It cracked her up.

"Why does he wear a hairnet?" she asked.

"He says it's what they wear in New York when they come out of prison," I said. "He wears it all the time."

Then I told her we were moving on. The line went silent. It was silent for a good few seconds. Then she asked where we were going.

"Out to the West Coast," I told her. "He thinks the idea's too big to work on here. We need a more professional studio. He works with a big producer out there, so we're taking it to him. It's going to be huge."

Silence again. Then she told me to fly her out there.

"Come on, Peacock," she said. "It's fucking freezing here. I want to see the sunshine. Come on, Peacock."

I told her I'd see what I could do. I told her there'd be a record company involved on the West Coast pretty soon and then we could afford it. I told her I'd sort it out.

"Don't let me down, Peacock," she said. "And don't take a detour through San Francisco with that wee jessy in his hairnet. Get me out there, Peacock. I mean it."

I hung up then. I'd had enough.

V

Let me tell you a wee bit about the wife. Jesus *Christ.*

Let me tell you.

First off, I know why it is she wants me to get her out to the West Coast. I know why that is. She's hoping she'll get to see Hollywood. Fucking Hollywood. That's her dream you know. She'd fucking love that.

I'll tell you what she'd have been doing when I phoned her this morning. It was raining and cold there, so I didn't have to ask her - I already knew. She'd be doing what she always does when it's raining and cold.

The first thing is a stupid big colourful cocktail. Bright green, or some unnatural neon blue, in a big fucking triangular glass. That's the first thing, but it's not the main thing. The main thing is what she'd be watching on TV, and there's no doubt about that. It would be black and white, from the Forties or Fifties - and more often than not starring Audrey Hepburn. Or that other cunt. Humphrey Bogart.

Whenever it's raining or cold, there she'll be - in the mid-afternoon - with her feet up on the coffee table, and her nuclear cocktail sitting on the arm of the chair.

I'm always telling her they only put that shite on in the middle of the afternoon because no one watches TV at that time of the day. So there's no point in them paying to make proper programmes that no one'll see.

But she sits there glued to it. Totally fucking transfixed.

And her dream is to go to Hollywood, to see where it all came from. I'm always trying to explain to her about that too. It's a tacky shite-hole, I tell her. Everyone knows that. Even I know that and I haven't been there. But she doesn't listen. She won't hear a fucking word spoken against it.

"If I ever got to go to Hollywood," she says on some of those afternoons, when the cocktails have started to turn her brain, "if I ever got to go there, I'll bet someone would discover me, Peacock. I'll bet someone would put *me* in a film like this."

"They don't *make* films like that anymore," I tell her. "It's all fucking Tom Cruise and digital fucking technology. They hardly even use actors anymore. It's all virtual computerisation."

"Ach..." she says, and closes her eyes - fucking swimming in alcohol.

I don't know what she thinks they'd discover about her either. She's a fucking looney.

So there you are. It's going to be a challenge thinking up reasons for why I can't bring her over, and trying to change the subject every time she brings it up on the phone. But at least I've got something to tell her about next time - to keep her off it. Wait till you hear about this. Wait till I tell you about the fucking stereo in the car. It's incredible.

For a start, it's none of that fucking cassette rubbish - it only takes CDs. And *how* it takes them. You put the disk part of the way into the slot, and then it takes it from you. Gently. Very gently. And the rest of the disk disappears into the machine.

But the most impressive thing happens after the CD starts playing. Me and Bob argued about that at first, he wouldn't even believe it was happening - but it was.

"Fuck me..." I said when I heard it. I didn't believe it myself straight away. I thought it must be some kind of coincidence.

"Slow down," I told the wee man.

"What?"

"Slow down."

"Why?"

"Just fucking do it."

So he did.

"Now speed up," I said.

"Fuck off."

"Speed up."

"What the fuck are you playing at, Peacock?"

"Speed *up*."

He sped up.

"Now slow down."

"You're fucking shitting me, man," he said.

"I'm not. Slow down and listen to the CD."

He looked at me with his eyes narrowed, then he slowed down.

"And speed up and listen to the CD."

"What the fuck *is* this shit?"

"Listen," I said.

"All I hear is you telling me to fucking speed up and slow down. What am I listening for?"

"When the engine gets louder the volume of the CD goes up. Automatically. When the engine gets quieter the volume goes back down again."

"Fuck off."

"It does."

"Does it fuck."

"It fucking does."

He gave me the narrow eyes again, but after a bit he started slowing down. Slowing down and speeding up. Speeding up and slowing down. Till even I was getting sick of it.

"Fuck..." he said in the end.

"Am I right?" I asked him.

"You're right, Peacock," he said. "You're fucking right. That's technology at its fucking peak. That's awesome."

"Alright," I told him. "Take it back to a steady speed now, son. You're starting to make me fucking seasick."

★

Portland. That's where we're headed. That's where the studio is, in Portland, Oregon. Further up the West Coast than LA.

I unfolded the map while we were stuck in traffic on the way out of Chicago, and I had a look at how far we had to go. It was a long fucking way. I took the top part of my finger to be about an inch, and I tried to work out how many miles it was.

"It'll take us about three or four days," Bob said. "We should make it to somewhere near Minneapolis tonight."

"It's quite a fucking country," I told him.

"In what way?"

"Four days? To get from one town to another? That's a big fucking place, son."

"It certainly is," he said, and then he asked me what highway we needed.

"I'm going to head for Wisconsin," he said. "What should I be on?"

I studied the map and worked it out.

"Highway 90," I told him.

"Highway 90..."

It took us a long time to get out of Chicago. The traffic was fucking terrible. But once we'd made it we got going good, and the fields just flew by.

"I'll tell you something else that's crazy about this country," Bob said then. "Something you're not going to like too much."

"What's that, son," I asked him.

"The State-lines," he said. "They can be awful. Security's pretty tight on them sometimes, and they like to make it difficult if you're not from the US."

We passed a sign that said: Wisconsin State-line, 10 Miles.

"I'll tell you what," Bob said. "They're really going to give you a fucking nightmare of a time, Peacock." And before I knew what he was doing the volume of the CD began to go down and he'd pulled onto the hard shoulder.

He turned the engine off and gave me a sly look.

"How about we smuggle you through," he said, and I asked him what the fuck he was talking about.

"Come here," he said, and he opened his door.

I followed him outside, and as we stood on the edge of the highway with all the traffic rushing past, he opened the boot of the car.

"Do you think you could handle that, Peacock?" he shouted at me, over the roar of the cars.

"I can fucking handle anything, son," I told him.

He slapped me on the back.

"It'll save us a lot of trouble," he said. "Otherwise we could be stuck there for hours. And then, of course, there's the rubber glove..."

I leapt into the boot of the car – or the fucking "trunk", as he called it. I leapt in and I curled up on my side.

"Keep your fingers crossed we can pull this off," he shouted, just before he slammed the boot shut, and I gave him a wee salute. Then it went dark. Pitch fucking dark.

It turned out to be a bad idea. A fucking *bad* idea. I don't know what speed he was doing with me in there, but I fucking bounced up and down till I thought every bone in my body was broken, and it felt more like fifty miles we'd travelled before the car stopped. Not ten.

I heard Bob's voice outside then, and I hoped the wee shite gave them the right answers. I got myself so tense I thought I was going to have a fucking heart attack lying there, waiting for the boot to open and some Yank guard to stick his gun in my face.

It was a relief when the car started moving again, but not for long. Those first ten miles had *seemed* like the longest trip of my life, but the next bit was worse. Much worse.

I bumped about so much my side would slam off the boot above me, then I'd slam back down and the other one would whack off the floor. I thought I was going to end up in hospital. And then I became convinced the air was running out.

Just before we stopped we seemed to be going round in tight circles and figure eights forever, and when Bob finally opened the boot I was lying all crumpled up in one corner.

The light was blinding at first.

"We made it, Peacock," he told me. "We fucking made it."

"You might have made it, son," I said. "I'm fucked."

But the cunt was laughing as I scrambled out of there.

"What's so fucking funny?" I asked him.

"Nothing," he said. "I'm just happy, Peacock. I'm just happy we got through."

We'd stopped outside a diner on a road that was just diners and fast food places and petrol stations, and Bob wanted to go in and get something to eat.

"Are you coming?" he asked me.

"Aye, just give me a minute, son," I told him. "Just let me sort myself out first."

I tried to straighten up my clothes, but they were a fucking mess. I don't like that. It gets me agitated when my clothes don't look good.

There was some kind of dirt from the boot on my trousers, and there were fucking wood shavings on my vest. I knocked off what I could, and then I went to comb my hair in the wing-mirror of the car.

"Come on," Bob shouted. "You look fine. Let's get something to eat, Peacock."

I walked up closer to him.

"Listen, wee man," I warned him. "Don't *ever* tell me I look fine when I don't. You might be happy to look like a fucking junkie-faggot, or whatever you call that look you've got. But I take a pride in my appearance, so just give me a fucking minute here, son."

Eventually we went inside. I still looked like a dog's fucking dinner, but I'd done what I could.

Still, it made me feel jumpy all the way through the meal.

"Where are we?" I asked Bob. He was eating what was supposed to be a grilled cheese sandwich, but it just looked like a fucking explosion to me. I hadn't taken any more chances. I'd ordered some bacon and some toast and made the fucking thing up myself.

"We're about ten miles into Wisconsin," Bob said. "I wanted

to drive far enough that no one would see you getting out."

"What's this town?"

"It's not a town. It's just a rest stop."

"I'll tell you what," I said to him. "I'm going to phone that idiot who put us together at my end, and I'm going to tell him he can forget his twenty per cent, considering he put me together with the wrong fucking guy."

"Thanks a lot," Bob said.

"No offence," I told him. "You know what I mean though, and there's no sense in paying a cunt. I'm just feeling a bit jumpy just now, I just need to go off at someone. I'll go and see if I can find a phone."

I was wishing I'd got my times wrong again, so's I could wake the cunt up at four in the morning, but he sounded pretty fresh.

"Peacock, man. How are you? How's the record going?"

"How am I? I'll tell you, you fucking prick. You've hooked me up with some cunt who knows as much about making a record as I do. Another guy with another idea, who came to Chicago under the impression that I could make *his* idea into a record. What the fuck are you playing at? You owe me fucking big time. *And* I'm going to kill you when I get back. You owe me for the flight, you owe me for hotels, and now I'm out on some fucking *road* trip - trying to find a guy who *can* help us make a record. And I'll tell you what, pal - you can forget about any twenty per cent when we do make one. *And* I'm going to fucking kill you. You owe me for a shite drum-machine box too. I'll tell you what I'm going to do to you when I get back. I'm going to..."

And then I stopped. Frozen. I dropped the phone, and from where it hung on its chord I could hear the wanker shouting,

"Peacock? Peacock? Are you there, pal? We can talk about this. Peacock? Are you there?"

I ran back to the table where Bob was sitting, and I grabbed him. "Get up," I said. "Get up."

The wee man looked bewildered, but he put some money on the table and got up. I dragged him to the door, and then to the car.

"We've got to go back," I told him. "We've got to go back."

"Why?"

"Come on, drive Bob. We've got to go back."

He started up the car, but he didn't get going.

"What's happening, Peacock?" he asked.

"The song," I said. "The fucking song. We left it on that fucking machine before we took it back to the shop."

He laughed. "Come on, Peacock..." he said.

"Come on, what? We left it on the fucking machine. Some fucker'll buy that and steal the idea. We've got to get it off there."

"But it was terrible. No one will even know what it's supposed to be."

"It's enough to put the idea in their head. I'm not arguing about it, Bob. We've got to go back."

He shook his head. He looked at me. Then he started driving. Once we were back out on the highway he shook his head again.

"How the fuck are we going to get it *off* the machine," he asked me.

I shrugged.

"You don't even *know*? This is insane, Peacock. I'm turning round."

"Keep going. We'll think of something."

"We'll have the record made before anyone buys that machine."

"We can't take that chance. Come on, keep going."

I got him convinced in the end that we had to do it, and then it was just a matter of working out how. We considered breaking in at night, but that would take time to plan. What we came up with was just as complicated in its way, but it would be quicker.

First of all we'd take the car back – say we'd changed our minds about the trip and get a refund. Then we'd use the money to buy the machine again.

Once we'd erased the song we'd take that back one more time – with the receipt – and then we'd hire the car again.

"It's a fucking nightmare plan," Bob said, when we had it sorted.

"It's a disaster," I agreed. "But it'll work. Just as long as we get the same machine back. And just as long as we get this same car. We *need* this CD player."

I relaxed then. I sat back in the seat, reclined it a wee bit, and put my hands behind my head. But I didn't stay like that for long. About a minute it must have been. Then I shot back up.

"You fucking *prick*," I shouted at Bob. Or screamed. And I hit him so hard that he let go of the steering wheel. Then he screamed.

"Peacock! You fucking maniac," he shouted. "What the fuck are you doing? You're going to fucking kill us."

"I'm going to fucking kill *you*," I told him.

"What the fuck for?" he said. "What the fuck's going on?"

The car had swerved pretty drastically, and I heard a lot of breaking going on around us.

"We're back in fucking *Illinois*," I shouted.

"So?"

"So where the fuck was the security on the State-line? We didn't even notice the fucking State-line. You made that whole thing up."

He looked around him till he saw a road sign.

"Shit," he said.

"What the fuck was the idea?"

"I don't like to be fucked with, Peacock," he told me. "That was for fucking with me in the hotel room. You were going to be in the trunk across every fucking State-line for that – all the way to fucking Portland."

He took his eyes off the road and started at me.

"Now you know how I work," he said.

And then he hit me back.

Fucking hard.

VI

The wife found it fucking hilarious, the idea of me in the boot. I told her: the *idea* might well be hilarious, but the reality of it was fucking hell.

I still can't believe the wee man would stoop to that.

Still, you've got to give him credit for having the balls to pull it off.

I looked fucking hellish when we got back to the hotel in Chicago. On top of the mess my clothes were in, I had a bruise on my cheek where he'd hit me, and I had to get changed as soon as we checked in. I just can't stand looking like that.

There was an iron in the room too, so I pressed up my fresh clothes to get rid of the suitcase creases. Then I started to feel better.

The wee man took care of getting a refund on the car, and buying the machine back. From what he told me the guy wasn't too keen to sell it to him again.

"What kind of game are you playing here?" he asked him.

"No game," Bob replied. "We just decided to give ourselves another chance. I think we were too hard on ourselves the first time."

When he got it back to the hotel he opened it up and tried to pretend to me it was a different machine, but it was the same one. Our song was on there, or our mess I should say.

We wiped off every last stinking note of it.

"So are you on the West Coast yet?" the wife asked me.

"We're back in fucking Chicago," I told her. I said something had gone wrong with the car, and we'd had to bring it back to get fixed.

"Let me fly out and meet you on the West Coast," she said.

I told her to fuck off.

"We're going to Portland, hen," I said. "It's further away from Hollywood than Glasgow is from Paris. I told you, once we get

36

set up with a record company and this record's a hit there'll be no problem, but I haven't got the money just now."

She went quiet. It fucking serves her right for laughing at the idea of me in the boot.

Fucking tart.

★

So the wee man somehow managed to return the machine and get the car back. He looked pretty knocked out when it was all done.

"How did you manage it?" I asked him.

"You don't want to know, Peacock," he said, and flopped down on the bed.

I would have been more surprised he'd got it done so quickly before the incident with the boot. But I was starting to see now that he didn't have that name for nothing.

"Let's get something to eat, Peacock," he said.

We'd decided not to set off again till the morning, so after some dinner we went down to the beach. It was on a lake apparently, Lake Michigan, but it looked more like the fucking sea to me. I mean, there are some pretty big Lochs in Scotland, but even then – you can always see the other side. This thing had a fucking horizon.

Still, it was fucking gorgeous, and it was a gorgeous evening too. It felt like the middle of summer, but it was only March.

"I read in the paper it's a freak heat wave," Bob said, as we walked a path along the edge of the lake. "It's brought them all out of hibernation anyway."

The place was fucking packed. Packed with joggers and speed-walkers and idiots like that. One guy passed us pushing a baby in a pram while he jogged.

"You're a freak," Bob shouted at him, as he ran past. "Yes, I mean you. Hey, buddy, you're a freak."

The guy turned round and Bob started laughing. Then another one, a speed-walker passed by, and Bob leant forward and shouted right into his ear.

"Freak! You're a freak, man."

That guy didn't turn around. He picked up his walk to an even faster pace, but Bob was cracking himself up. He moved out into the main flow of them all; cyclists, cunts on roller boots, the joggers and the funny walkers, and he spread his arms out like wings – and started turning round slowly. I stood and watched the chaos he was causing, as everyone tried to flow round about him and avoid each other.

"Freaks!" he shouted. "Freaks!"

Then he started pretending he was trying to grab people as they went past, and he started laughing even harder.

Eventually he staggered out of there and flopped down onto the grass, gasping for breath as he laughed.

"Freak," he shouted at one more guy, and then he stood up and brushed himself down.

"Ah," he said. "I enjoyed that. Freaks! Freaks. What a life, eh? Come on, Peacock. Let's go and find a drink."

We looked for bars all the way between there and the hotel, but there wasn't a single one. So we ended up back in the bar at the hotel.

Bob started laughing again as he sat down with the drinks. "That was a riot," he said, and he pushed my beer towards me.

"There you go, Peacock," he said. "It's party time." And he asked if he'd told me about his first real job.

"You told me you were with the Boston Ballet," I reminded him.

"Ah, but that wasn't my first job," he said. "I worked there, but my first job was as a professional party boy."

"A what? What the fuck is that?" I asked him. "Is that like a rent boy?"

"What's a rent boy?"

"A prostitute. Like a male prostitute."

"Fuck off," he said. "I was a party boy. Someone paid me to work in their club, and I'd go around just talking to the customers, getting as much free drink as I wanted."

I laughed.

"It sounds to me like you misunderstood them, pal. It sounds to me like you were supposed to be prostituting in there. Was it a gay club?"

"Fuck off, Peacock," he said. "It was just a club, and that was my job. Partying. It was the best job in the world for a while, but I couldn't keep it up. It would have killed me."

"How long did you do it?"

"Eighteen months."

"Eighteen months as a prostitute, eh?"

"I wasn't a fucking prostitute. I'll tell you what though; I'm in the mood for a party tonight."

"A party? We couldn't even find a bar, wee man."

"I can always find a party," he said.

But he didn't. We had a couple more beers and then went back to our rooms.

"We should have been in Minneapolis tonight," Bob said, on the way up in the lift. "I'd have found us a party there. You can always find a party in Minneapolis."

"You can find us one tomorrow night," I told him.

"I will," he said. "You watch me. We should have been there tonight. No one would have stolen that song."

But I was glad we'd come back and got it off the machine. It meant I could relax properly again. When I got to my room I lay down and turned on the TV, and I found a magic programme on there – some guy fishing for big-mouthed bass in Canada. And he caught them too.

I got another beer from the mini-bar and settled down to enjoy it properly. I fucking love fishing programmes. I like watching them at home, but this stuff was much more spectacular. And when it finished another one started. It was like a whole channel just dedicated to fishing programmes.

I was in my fucking element.

VII

If anything, the weather was even better the next day. It wasn't much later than ten o'clock when we climbed into the car, but the sun was already blazing.

"You're dressed for the weather," Bob said to me, and he was right. I'd the vest off, and I was wearing my Hawaiian shirt open. I'd put on my Hawaiian shorts too, and I was wearing the beach flip-flops.

"Have you got everything with you?" he asked me. "You haven't left anything behind this time? No bits of paper by the bed with the idea for your next hit on it? No thoughts floating about in the room that might invade someone else's head?"

"Fucking drive," I told him, and he laughed. Then we were off.

I rolled the window down and stuck my head outside. The breeze felt good and I took a look at myself in the wing-mirror. That bruise was almost gone. The wee man wasn't as hard a hitter as I'd given him credit for.

"What's all this shit written on here?" I asked him. " 'Objects in the rear view mirror may be closer than they appear.' That's a fucking Meatloaf song."

"Pretty much," Bob said.

"What's it written on there for?"

"To prevent accidents."

"To prevent them? The way I see it, you'd take a look in there, start trying to read that, and then hit the car in front."

"Put the window up, Peacock," he said. "It's starting to get too hot in here."

"That's why it's down," I told him.

"Put it up."

"It's too fucking hot."

He pushed a button and forced it up. I tried to open it again, but it wouldn't move.

"What the fuck are you doing?" I asked him. But then,

gradually, it got cooler inside.

"What's going on," I said.

"Air-conditioning," he explained. "When the windows are closed we've got complete control of the temperature in here."

I looked at him.

"This country is finally starting to impress me," I said, and I told him all about the fishing programmes, but that didn't seem to impress him too much.

We stopped for lunch in a place called Madison – a bit further into Wisconsin than we'd got the day before. It was a nice place. Bob stocked up on some magazines at an adult book store, and I got myself a fine pair of trousers in a second-hand place. A wide flare and a stylish check. "They don't make them like . that anymore, son. They fucking should, but they don't."

We sat in the sun for a while before we left, just soaking it up.

"I think I'm going to enjoy this trip," I told Bob. "The weather's fucking incredible."

"I'd enjoy it a lot more if you could drive," he said. "It'd be quicker too. One of us could sleep while the other one drove. That's the way to do this shit. No need for motels either."

"Relax," I told him. "It'll be fine. Just fucking take it easy."

We bought an Elvis CD on the way back to the car, just to give old Glen a rest. We'd been playing him constantly since we got the car, and I didn't want to wear the guy out.

"Spark that up," I told Bob, as he flicked through one of his magazines. Then I reclined my seat and we were off again.

The road was wide and open from there, and as we travelled I felt my eyes getting heavy and I reclined the seat further. The next thing I knew the wee man was bumping me on the arm and welcoming me to Minneapolis. I'd been out like a light for the whole fucking trip.

★

"Wake up," Bob said, and I groaned. "Come on, baby. We're

here."

Slowly, I released the seat from its recline and Minneapolis came into view. The seat had come up gently, but when it reached its limit I threw myself forward with a much more powerful force.

I looked around me.

"What the *fuck*..." I said.

"You like it?"

"What the fuck is going on?" I asked him, and I watched as a car passed us in the outside lane - with six inch *icicles* hanging from its under-carriage. All the verges were feet deep in snow.

"Where is this really?" I asked him. "Fucking Russia?"

He laughed. "It's Minneapolis," he said.

"What temperature is it out there?"

He shrugged, then he pointed.

We were passing a sign with an electronic display, which changed back and forwards between the time: 19:56, and the temperature: 20 degrees fahrenheit.

"Twenty *degrees*?"

"That's what it says."

"*Twenty*? It was fucking *eighty* in Chicago. What's twenty degrees in centigrade? How far is that below freezing?"

"What am I, Peacock? A fucking weatherman? Let's just say it's cold. Maybe minus ten. It's fucking cold, baby."

"And stop fucking calling me that, Bob. Where the fuck did that come from? Is this some kind of weird fucking dream? It must be. It fucking must be. I fall asleep and it's summer, and then... *this*. And into the bargain you've started calling me baby? It's a dream, isn't it? A sick fucking dream."

"Relax, Peacock," Bob said. "Relax. I'm just excited. I'm getting into party mode. I call everyone baby in party mode."

"Well don't call *me* it."

"Okay, okay. Just relax about the fucking weather."

"*Relax*? How the fuck can I relax? *Look* at me, Bob," I pointed down at my clothes. "I'm dressed for the fucking *beach*," I said.

42

Bob laughed.

"You could have fucking warned me," I told him.

"That you were dressed for the beach?"

"That it would be like this."

"I didn't know, Peacock," he said. "I told you already, I'm not a fucking weatherman."

We found a hotel and Bob drove around in the snow in the car park. I told him to get a space as close to the door as he could, but there was nothing. He had to park about two hundred yards away.

"I'll run across and see if they have rooms," he said. And when he came back - nodding - he was fucking blue.

"We're in," he said, and ran round to open the boot.

I got out and grabbed my case. There were three inches of snow on the ground and I was in my fucking bare feet and flip-flops.

"Run," Bob said. "Before we fucking die."

So I ran, slipping about like a cunt behind him. And then it happened. I hit a big mound of ice and went up on my fucking arse - suitcase skidding across the car park, and one beach shoe up in the air. Then I heard a shout. The suitcase had caught Bob from behind, and knocked him backwards. And he ended up on his arse too.

We were a big fucking hit by the time we reached reception. Everyone in the lobby had been watching us through the windows.

Laurel and fucking Hardy.

"I see this wasn't the weather you were expecting," the guy at the desk said as he checked me in.

I didn't fucking answer. I knew how it would go. I'd say something and he'd say, "What?" and then "What?!" Then I'd swear under my breath and - miraculously - he'd hear that. Then the aggro, then the fucking gun.

It wasn't fucking worth it, so I kept my mouth shut.

"How's the back?" I asked Bob on the way up in the lift.

"Alright," he said. "That was quite a fucking shot, Peacock, but I'm alright. How are you?"

I nodded. "I'm okay, son," I told him. "I'll be fine once I get changed."

The lift slammed to a halt at our floor, and we got out.

The old couple getting in stared at me like I was a fucking mental patient.

"Evening," I said. "It's turned out nice now."

They looked at each other and scurried inside, hurriedly pressing buttons.

Bob started cracking up. "I'll come and get you in about twenty minutes," he said.

"No bother, son," I told him. "I'll go and see if there's any of that fishing on TV."

★

Now, from there on in Minneapolis starts to become a bit of a blur. I had a couple of beers from the mini-bar while I watched the fishing programme, and a couple more while they served me a fucking enormous rack of ribs at the noisiest fucking restaurant in the world.

I can remember that alright.

I can remember me and Bob causing a bit of a fuss trying to get them to turn down the speaker above our table in there. And I don't think I'll ever forget that fucking rack of ribs. It must have been two feet long. But the rest of the evening - we've been trying our best to piece that together between us. And Bob has a bit more piecing to do than me, quite a bit more. Cause when I went to his room late this morning he wasn't there, and he still wasn't back when it was time to check-out.

I sat in the lobby with my case and my spectacular hangover and no fucking clue about what to do. An hour later he still wasn't there, and they sent me up with a key to get his stuff out of the room, so's they could clean it for the next person.

I was just reaching the terrible crossroads of having to pick up his underwear from the floor, when he came through the door and collapsed onto the bed.

"Oh, fuck..." he said.

"Where have you *been*?" I asked him.

"Oh, no..." he said. "Fuck."

"We've got to go," I told him. "If we don't get out they're going to charge us another night for the room. Come on, party boy."

He groaned and sat up on the bed.

"Come on," I said. "Put that stuff in the bag."

I checked out for him while he shakily took the bags to the car.

"I see you're dressed more appropriately today," the guy at the desk laughed. "That's a very nice jacket, sir."

"Cheers, pal," I said. "I like it."

I fucking love it. I think they call it an Afghan coat - brushed suede with sheepskin lining and a sheepskin collar. It took me fucking ages to find one, and it cost a bomb too. But there's a fucking stain on it now that worries me, from that night. I'm hoping the wife can get it out.

Bob looked terrible when I got to the car. It seemed to cause him pain just to put the seat-belt on.

"Alright," he said then. "Coffee. We need coffee, Peacock. Let's go."

VIII

Ill as Bob was, we drove a long way that day; all the way through Minnesota, and halfway into North Dakota, where we stayed in a place called Bismark. We made a lot of coffee stops along the way, and after the first hour - when Bob just stared at the road with the widest fucking eyes I'd ever seen, and didn't say a single word - we started to do a lot of piecing together.

He broke his long silence by shaking his head.

"Oh, God..." he said. "Fuck I feel bad."

"Where did you end up?" I asked him.

"I don't know where it was," he said. "Somewhere way out in the suburbs."

I'd no memory of coming back to the hotel, and neither of us could remember where we'd left each other.

"I woke up on the arm of a chair," Bob said. "Sitting in this house somewhere. There were about ten other people sleeping in the room, and I saw a couple of girls sleeping on the floor. Then I remembered I'd come there with them."

"Two of them, eh?" I laughed. "You *are* the party boy."

"Oh fuck..." he said. "Oh no... I'm remembering something, Peacock. Something bad. Oh..."

"Something you did?"

"Something *we* did."

I looked at him.

"No," he said. "No... Go away."

"What the fuck is it?" I asked him.

"You don't want to know. Maybe it's just a false memory."

"Tell me," I said.

"You remember the first club we were in?" he asked.

"Remind me."

"It had different levels. It was all dark, with shitty laser lights, and people dancing on the stairs."

I could see that, vaguely.

"Do you remember we left there and went looking for a bar?"

That was a lot less clear to me.

"We found a smaller place," Bob said. "You'll remember. You'll remember us watching a small stage in the corner of the room and laughing."

I didn't remember it at all, but I could feel something unpleasant struggling to the surface - as if I'd lifted a big fucking brick and an ugly creature that lived under there was scuttling to escape.

"Do you remember?" he asked me.

"I'm trying not to," I said. "But it doesn't feel good."

46

"It's not good, Peacock," he said. "It's not good at all."

He screwed his face up, and then he told me. I felt it like a sharp pain and I winced.

"Ouch," I said.

"We don't want to talk about this ever again, Peacock," he said to me. "Fuck knows what else we did if we did that."

I'll tell you what we did.

We did karaoke.

Bob decided not to drink any more coffee for a while, in case it brought anything else back. But I was already having a wee recollection of my own. I was remembering that we hadn't *left* that first club, we'd been thrown out of it. I'd got us thrown out of it.

The music had suddenly changed from some pretty heavy dance stuff to a Prince song, 'The Most Beautiful Girl In The World', and we'd been standing next to this fucking gorgeous bird at the time.

I asked Bob if any of that came back to him, and unfortunately it did.

"What was I shouting at her?" I asked him, and he did a really bad impression of me.

"Hey, darlin'. Darlin'. This is you, pal. This song, this is you."

And she'd moved away, and I went behind her - through the crowd of dancers - while she tried to pretend I wasn't there.

"Hey, darlin'," Bob shouted now, cracking himself up. "Come back, doll. I'm saying, that's you. This song. That's you."

"I don't think I'll bother telling the wife about that," I said to him. "Still, you were the lucky one - eh? *Two* birds."

He shook his head.

"When we got back to that house they both had boyfriends there. I think I sat on the arm of that chair all night - trying to survive the drugs they'd given me."

I laughed.

"I wonder what we sang at the karaoke," I said.

"I'm sure we'll remember soon enough," Bob sighed. "It all

comes back in the end."

But I didn't agree.

"There are things I've never fucking remembered," I told him.

"Never?"

I shook my head. "There's one night the wife's always banging on about, but I can't remember a fucking thing about it."

"What happened?" Bob asked.

So I told him.

I'd been playing cards at a mate's house, and we'd got totally fucking legless. Drunk stupid. And the wife tells me he walked over home with me, and we had a few more drinks there. Then, apparently, I decided it'd be rude to let him walk back on his own, so I saw him over to his place. And we kept on like that. Back and forward, back and forward. Fuck knows for how long.

Bob laughed.

"That's only the half of it, though," I said, and I told him the rest.

Eventually his wife managed to persuade him to let me go back on my own. Either that or he was finally too drunk to walk anymore. But a while after I'd left, his wife phoned mine to check I'd made it back okay, and I hadn't. So the wife and a neighbour came out looking for me, and they found me on the bridge across the river. I was over to the side on a bit that was closed off, with one leg dangling through a hole where the wood had crumbled. And I was fast a-fucking-sleep.

"Asleep?" Bob said.

"Asleep, son. Twenty feet above the river. Apparently they dragged me out of there and shouldered me home, but I've never remembered any of it."

"Nothing?"

"Not a bit," I told him. "Mind you, there's no way in hell the wife'll ever let me forget it."

IX

It took us two more days, and two monster drives, to get from Bismark to Portland. The first day was pretty boring. The road was straight to the horizon, and it was long, and we stopped late that night in Butte, Montana – where we had a few drinks before we slept, mostly to help the wee man calm down.

He'd got a bit of a fright along the way. Still, it was his own fucking fault. He'd kept moaning all the way along that straight road about how straight it was. And then he'd started in on me.

"I fucking wish you could drive, Peacock," he said. "What's wrong with you, man? Why can't you drive?"

"Oh, I can drive," I told him. "I haven't got a licence, but I can drive."

I told him I'd take over next time we stopped if he wanted, but he said I couldn't take over if I didn't have a licence. He was driving me fucking crazy, though – driving me mental with his constant moaning. He was starting to sound like a fucking woman. So at the next stop I grabbed the keys from him at the table, and I put them in my pocket.

"Come on, Peacock," he said. "Give them back. You can't drive here without a licence. We'll both end up in prison."

But I didn't answer him. He reached over the table a couple of times while we ate, and tried to grab at my pocket – but I knocked him away.

"Will you stop moaning about driving if I give you them back?" I asked him.

"I'll stop," he said.

"Alright. Then I'll give them back."

"Thanks, Peacock," he said. "All I've been saying is it'd be easier if we could both drive. It's a hard fucking gig doing this all on your own."

I sighed.

"Bob..." I said

"What?"

"You're fucking moaning again. I told you, I'm going to help you out. Just sit back and relax, son. Enjoy your lunch."

I was already in the driving seat when he got outside, but he wouldn't get in.

"Hurry up," I told him. "I'll fucking leave you here."

"Get out, Peacock," he shouted. "Give me the fucking keys. You can't..."

So I started driving away. Not too fast, just enough to let him run after me.

It was a fucking easy car to drive. No gears. Nothing. I kept going for a bit, with him still running behind me, then I stopped and let him catch up.

"Are you getting in?" I asked him.

"That's enough. Peacock," he said. "Let me drive now."

I moved off again, faster this time. And when I looked in the mirror I could see him standing with his hands in the air, defeated.

"Shit," he said, as he climbed in.

But I can drive. I can drive fine. I just haven't passed the test, and a child could have driven this car. Stop and go - that's all there was to it. And once you got up to a certain speed you just hit the cruise thing and it drove itself. All I had to do was steer. I couldn't work out what all his complaining had been about.

I was making a lot better time than he'd made too. He'd spent most of the journey sitting around seventy, seventy-five. But I had us up to ninety in no time. I turned that cruise thing on around ninety-five, and weaved us in and out of all the cars that were crawling along. I moved from lane to lane.

His fucking moaning got to be more unbearable than it had been when he'd been driving though. And at least when he'd been driving his moaning hadn't been all panicky too. Every time I looked round at him he looked paler than the time before, and there were times when he even stooped to letting out a wee squeal, when I moved us from one lane to another to pass the next fucking kerb-crawler.

"Enough, Peacock," he shouted a couple of times. "Enough."

You'd have thought he was on the fucking waltzers, and he kept saying if we passed a cop car we'd be finished. But what the fuck would a cop car be doing out there in the middle of nowhere. Nothing, that's what.

But I decided in the end to give it up anyway, cause his moaning was worse than when he drove – so I wasn't achieving anything. And it was just getting me agitated.

I saw a sign for more petrol stations and fast food places and decided to stop there. The road swung round on a long bend towards the exit, and I followed it along. I suppose I didn't slow down enough for it though, cause the back wheels moved out from underneath us and the car whipped round. That took us over onto the other side of the road and across the lanes there, and we came to a stop at the top of the embankment, but it was alright. The road was empty coming that way, and it was fine.

We'd come to a neat fucking stop too, facing the opposite way from the way we'd been going.

"You fucking *maniac*," Bob started shouting. "You're fucking *insane*, Peacock. Get out of the car. Get out. Get into this fucking seat *now*."

He went pretty mental. I laughed a bit and got out. He started pushing me about at the top of the embankment.

"You almost fucking killed us," he shouted. "You crazy fucking bastard."

"Calm down," I told him, but he kept pushing me. Then he tripped over something and knocked his full weight onto me, and the two of us took a tumble down the embankment into a field.

"For fuck sake," I shouted. "Get a grip on yourself, son."

I tried dragging him back up to the road, but he was throwing this crazy wee tantrum, and he kept kicking and pulling. Then he started tumbling all the way back down the embankment and into the field again.

I climbed up to the top and looked down at him. He was just lying there on his back with his arms and legs out in the shape of a star.

"Come on," I shouted at him. "Get up."

He didn't answer for a bit and then, still without moving, still lying on his back, he let out pretty much the loudest shout I'd ever heard. It seemed to echo all through the place. Just one word.

"Bastard."

So I got him those few drinks after he'd driven us to Butte, just to help calm him down. And some good did come out of the whole thing. He didn't moan once about having to drive the next day, or about me not being able to drive. He was as bright as a button, and we had a good time.

There was plenty to see too.

Driving out of Butte there was an enormous statue of the Virgin Mary up on the mountain. It was a fucking spectacular sight. But nothing compared to the landscape we drove through later.

There was one place where we stopped at a viewpoint, and it was fucking incredible. It looked down on an enormous gorge through the desert, with a river running through it – and we were up high in the brown rocks – and higher up still there were these fucking mental sculptures of cowboys on horses. It was fucking bizarre.

We drove through more desert, and then suddenly we were in a landscape that looked like fucking Austria – all green and trees and mountains. I was fucking glad not to be driving – there was too much to look at.

So that was a good day, and it was another long day too. We got to Portland around midnight, five fucking days after we'd set out. Admittedly we hadn't got anywhere on the first day, but it was a long fucking time to sit in a car, and I was fucking glad to be there.

"Well," Bob said, as we went up to our rooms. "This is the place, Peacock. This is where it's going to happen. That was one long fucking trip."

I nodded.

He shook his head.

"You done well," I told him.

"I'm fucking drained," he said.

"You'll be alright," I told him. "What happens tomorrow?"

"I phone the guy who knows the guy out here, and I'll find out when we can go and meet him."

"Sounds good," I said.

The lift stopped on our floor.

"Get some rest, wee man," I told him, and I went to find my own room. Then I wondered about what I'd just said. "Sounds good"? Fuck me, I thought. I've been in this country too long. Next thing I know I'll have a fucking gun.

X

"Fucking freedom," Bob said, as we walked out of the hotel the next morning. And he raised his middle finger at our car parked on the street.

It did feel good just to be walking around, and to know we weren't going to have to spend the whole day sitting down again.

We found a place for breakfast, and Bob told me about the phone call he'd made to his guy.

"It's all happening," he said. "He kept going on about where the fuck had we been for the last two days. He thought we'd be here sooner. But it's cool. The guy here didn't want us to come along to his place till today anyway, so I don't know what the fuck all the fuss was about."

"Is it far from here?"

"Not too far. I've got directions. P.O. Productions. We've to go there about four."

"Four? What the fuck are we going to do till then?"

"I don't know. Just see the place. Eat some good food instead of that roadside garbage we've been eating all week. Have a few drinks..."

As it turned out, we leant more towards the drinks idea than the good food one. And we got ourselves into a wee spot of trouble. Not too much, mind you – just a spot. And that was before we'd even had a drink.

When we'd finished breakfast we were walking around a bit, trying to work out what to do, and Bob went across to a shop to buy some cigarettes. I didn't cross over with him, just stayed where I was, and I saw two guys starting to follow him.

You can usually tell when someone's thinking about doing some mugging, but these guys weren't thinking about that. They were considering his potential for something else entirely.

"Watch your arse, Bob," I shouted, and that upset them. They swung around on me then.

"I'm sorry, guy," one of them said, all flapping wrists and perfume. "We didn't know he was taken, honey."

"Boy is you protective," the other one said.

"But that's nice," the first one interrupted. "I like that. A good, strong man."

And he reached out a hand to touch the top of my arm. I knocked it away.

"What the fuck are you doing?" I asked him.

"Oh boy, they *is* close," the second one said.

"Very close," the first one agreed. "Where are you from, honey? That's a lovely accent you have."

I'll be honest with you here – I started to wish they had been muggers. I had no fucking idea how to handle the situation. With muggers it would have been easy, you don't even have to think about it. You just get stuck right in – then you take everything off them that they've taken from other people. I didn't even know what these guys were doing.

Luckily Bob came out of the shop then, and he crossed back over.

He shook his head at me.

"Listen, guys," he said. "This is Peacock. Peacock Johnson. He's from Scotland. He's over here travelling and I'm showing him around. My name's Bob."

He shook hands with them, then said he apologised for my behaviour.

"This is his first time here," he said.

Fuck knows how, but that seemed to work. In a way.

"That's a beautiful name, honey," the first one said to me. "Well, you enjoy your stay here."

"And both of you enjoy each other," the second one said.

Then they were leaving, waving at us both as they went.

"You stupid fuck," Bob whispered at me, as he waved back to them.

"What?"

"You can't shout shit like that, Peacock."

"But it didn't look good," I told him.

"I know. But how good did it look after you shouted?"

"Worse."

"Alright."

I saw what he meant.

"Don't try anything like that again, Peacock," he said, and I assured him I wouldn't. Then we went off to find somewhere we could get a drink and forget about it.

So we'd had a few by the time we went off to meet our guy, but we were alright. We got a taxi there, in case we got lost – and it dropped us at an entrance with the names of a few companies by the door.

"There it is," Bob said, pointing. "P. O. Productions. Second Floor."

P. O. Productions was written in big letters – and below it, in smaller ones, were the words "Portland, Oregon Productions."

"Fucking imaginative," I muttered, and off we went to the lift.

I wasn't sure if stairs existed in America, but I certainly hadn't seen any in the time I'd been there.

When we found the place a pretty fucked-up looking guy answered the door, and I hoped he wasn't ours.

"We're looking for Ray Stewart," Bob told him, and he turned round. I started breathing more easily when he shouted to someone else.

He brought us into an office where you could hardly move for boxes on the floor. Stacked boxes, scattered boxes - and then he pointed us to another door, and we knocked on that.

"Come in," the voice shouted, and I assumed that was Ray. And when we got inside Ray didn't look too fucked-up at all.

"Hi guys," he said. "How can I help you?"

Bob leant forward to shake his hand.

"I'm Bob," he said. "This is Peacock."

Ray's face lit up.

"My music men," he said. "How are you both?"

"Good," Bob said. "Good."

"Aye, fine son."

"Excellent. Excellent... Frank!" he shouted, and the fucked-up guy put his head round the door.

"Get us some coffees, would you? Do you guys want some coffee? I need some coffee. Okay, let me see here."

He looked around for something in a drawer then tidied more things off his desk.

"Alright," he said. "So how was the trip? That was a long way you guys came."

"It wasn't too bad," Bob told him. "We made it."

"Aye," I said. "We got here, son."

"I'm glad you did. Very glad. Ah, here's the coffee. Excellent. So - Michael speaks very highly of you both. I'm looking forward to this, I really am."

"So are we," Bob said, and I wondered who the fuck Michael was, to be speaking so highly of me. I assumed he must be Bob's guy.

"I imagine he's filled you in on what I do," Ray said. "I've got all the equipment ready and waiting. Everything's just about set."

"And you know what we've got planned?" Bob asked.

"Just whatever you guys want to do," Ray said. "I'm totally open. I trust you guys entirely."

He took a big drink from his coffee and then started scribbling down on a piece of paper.

"Here's the address of the place," he said while he wrote. "And I'll put some directions on here too, so you guys can find it alright."

When he was finished he pushed it across the table to us.

"So I'll see you guys there around eight," he said. "Does that sound good?"

"It sounds great, pal," I told him - and then the fucked-up guy showed us out.

XI

We drank a bit more, waiting to go along to the place at eight, but we did manage to fit some of the good food in this time too. And it was fucking great food - in a restaurant not far from the hotel. It helped soak up some of the drink, and we weren't too bad by the time we got to the place.

It seemed the place was mainly a club, but when we asked for Ray someone took us through to the back, and Ray was hurrying about in there.

"Ah, guys - guys..." he said, and he went into a drawer again - then he came towards us and put a hand on my back.

"Okay, come with me," he said, and took us back the way we had come.

As we walked he held out an envelope and asked who wanted to take it. He held it out first to Bob, then to me - then he shrugged and gave it to Bob.

We were back into the club by then, and he took us over to a corner.

"Here's all the equipment," he said. "Everything's here. Just so long as you guys have the records."

He laughed, and patted Bob on the back.

"You guys settle in here," he said. "I've got to get a few last minute things ready, and then I'll be back." He pointed at the envelope. "That's how you wanted it, right? Half now and half later?"

Then he fucked off.

I frowned at Bob and Bob frowned at me.

"What the fuck is that?" I asked him.

He shrugged and I took it from him.

I opened it.

"Jesus," I said. "Look at that, Bob."

It was full of fucking money. A lot of money.

"What the fuck's going on?" Bob said, and he started counting it. Then he stopped – he stopped suddenly – and he pointed at something behind me.

"Cunt..." he said.

He was pointing at a poster on the wall, and on the poster it said: "Evil Bob and Peacock Johnson – International DJs. Club ISIS. March 14th – 8.30pm til late."

"How come your name's before mine?" I asked him.

"*What?*" he shouted. "What the fuck are you *talking* about, Peacock. What are we going to *do*?"

"How much is in the envelope?" I asked him, and he started counting it again. Then he looked up.

"A thousand dollars," he whispered.

"Okay," I said. "Let's go."

"Go?"

I nodded.

"Put it in your pocket and we'll just walk out of here. Then we'll go and fucking kill that cunt of yours."

He folded up the envelope.

"Hang on though," I said, and I thought for a bit. "If we actually do this – didn't he say 'Half now, half later'? That's another grand..."

"*Do* it? How the fuck are we going to manage that?"

"How hard can it be?"

"Hard. We haven't got any fucking *records*, Peacock. I liked your first plan better. Let's just get out of here."

I stopped him.

"There's a record shop right across the road," I told him. "I saw it on the way in. A second-hand place. Go and get some records and I'll figure out how all this stuff works."

"This is madness, Peacock," he said. "Let's just fucking go."

"It's another grand," I told him. "Go and buy some fucking records."

"No."

"Go."

"Fuck off."

Ray came over then. He gave us a great big smile.

"How are you guys doing?" he asked. "Things going smoothly?"

"Perfectly," I told him, then I turned to Bob. "The wee man's just off to get the rest of the records from the car," I said, and the wee man gave me a murderous look. And off the wee man went.

I didn't have long to bask in my fucking victory, though. A few seconds later I was cursing the wee bastard's luck. It started with Ray's hand on my shoulder.

"Alright," he said. "We're going with doors in five. Are you guys ready to go? There's a crate of beer for you there in the booth. If you need anything else, just let me know."

And then he was gone again. He had quite a talent for disappearing it seemed. And a couple of minutes later all the fucking lights went off. All I'd had time to do was open a beer, and now I couldn't see a fucking thing. I fumbled around in the booth trying to feel things, and luckily I stumbled on a wee light. I pointed it around and tried to work out how to switch things on, then I looked up. The place was nearly fucking full already. I nearly fucking shat myself. I couldn't work out where in fuck they'd all come from so quickly, and I knew it would take Bob fucking ages to get back.

I looked at what was there. Two record decks and a space age CD player, and some other fucking complicated looking thing with knobs and sliders on it. I started to sweat. I unbuttoned the Afghan, and started taking it off – and that's when I was saved. There was something in there – something bulging in the pocket, and my heart fucking leapt. It was the big man. Glen fucking Campbell. To the rescue again.

I managed to get the weird CD player open and I slammed it in there. Then I found a switch on the complicated looking thing that said "CD" and I sparked it up. And on it came, blasting out through the club, 'Dreams of the Everyday Housewife.'

I was fucking thrilled. It probably wasn't what they were expecting to hear in there, but it was fucking music all the same.

Good fucking music.

★

By the time Bob got back I'd gone through 'Galveston', 'Guess I'm Dumb' and 'Country Boy'. I was just trying to decide what to give them next when he came staggering back into the booth under the most enormous stack of LPs I'd ever fucking seen. They were piled up so high in his arms that only his eyes were showing over the top.

"What the fuck's going on here?" he asked me, as he tipped them down onto the floor.

"We've started, son," I told him.

"I can see that, but what the fuck are you playing?"

"Glen."

"Glen Campbell? Jesus Christ, Peacock. Help me find something else in here quickly. You can't play Glen Campbell at a night like this."

"It's going alright," I told him. "Have a beer. That whole crate's for us. Free."

He shuffled about amongst his records and then looked out over the top of the booth.

"What the fuck gave you the idea that it's going alright?" he asked me. "Have you looked out there?"

"I haven't had time, son," I told him.

"Well take a look now."

I had to admit they all looked pretty confused. There were certainly a lot of them, but most of them were standing staring at our booth.

"Hurry up," Bob said. "Help me find something in here."

So I got down onto the floor with him and started rummaging around.

"How much did all this cost you?" I asked him.

"Practically nothing," he said. "I just grabbed everything from the fifty cents bin."

It fucking showed. He'd got a lot of shite. I certainly couldn't find anything in there that was going to be an improvement on what we were already playing. To start with, about half of it was classical.

"Fucking hell," I said, and Bob scrambled about – pulling out heavy metal records and recordings of American poets. Then he jumped up.

"Alright," he said. "This'll do to start with."

He'd found a compilation of TV funk themes from the 70's, and he slammed it onto one of the decks.

"How does this work?" he asked me.

I moved the switch on the thing from 'CD' to 'Phono 1'. Glen had just been starting up 'Gentle On My Mind', but that put paid to him.

"Jesus, Peacock," Bob said. "That was fucking smooth."

But he was one to talk. He put the needle down and the song sparked up half way through. Then the needle skidded across a scratch, and came to a rest just before the start of the next song.

"Have a beer," I told him, when the next song started. "We'll let this side play through."

I opened one for him, but after one slug he was straight back down onto the floor, hunting amongst the records.

He found one compilation of chart hits from the 80's, and when the TV themes reached the end of that side he put it on, and alternated one song about between that and the second side of the funky TV stuff.

I'll tell you – there wasn't a lot else in there. We had to get through the four hours from there till the end of the night with just a Brazilian Carnival album, the soundtrack from *Grease*, and a Jane Fonda workout record – skipping it as best we could over her exercise instructions between the songs.

If you do the sums you'll realise that just doesn't add up to four hours. It leaves a lot of extra time.

To fill some of it Bob managed a wee bit of genius. He'd noticed that one of the songs on the TV themes started just with drums, and he said he'd heard you could keep winding a record back to keep the same bit playing over again. So he practiced that on the free deck through the headphones, until he thought he could do it okay. And when the record on the other deck finished I turned the switch to play that one.

To be honest, it didn't really sound that good. He was getting it right some of the time, and wrong some of the time. But mostly it was just nearly right, and it didn't sound great.

Still, it didn't look as bad as earlier out front. I had a wee peek out over the booth, and most of the people weren't staring at it anymore – they were facing in all different ways, talking and drinking. A few of them were even trying their best to dance to Bob's fucked-up drums.

"Peacock!" he shouted at me then.

"What?"

"Get one of those classical records and find out how to make both decks play at once."

I looked at him.

"Go on," he said. "It might work. We can't keep this fucking drumbeat playing all night on its own."

So I put one on. Most of the time it didn't fit in with the drums at all, but occasionally they came together.

We probably kept on with that for longer than we should have, about half an hour in all. But then Bob started to get a cramp in his hand, and it all seized up in a weird fucking spasm. He let the record go then, and the funk started playing along with the classical, and I made a quick grab for the classical one and pulled it off.

"Fucking Jesus," Bob shouted, flapping his hand about.

I opened him another beer.

"I'll tell you what we should do," I shouted at him.

"What should we do, Peacock?" he said. "What's your next fucking master plan?"

"We should finish up with some more Glen," I told him. "Give the evening some coherence."

"*Coherence*? What the fuck are you, an *artist* now?"

But he couldn't really argue, cause we had fuck-all else left to play.

I put on 'By The Time I Get To Phoenix' and 'Rhinestone Cowboy', and just as I started 'Reason to Believe' the lights came up. We'd fucking made it.

I shook Bob's spastic hand.

"No bother, wee man," I said to him. "No fucking bother at all."

PART II

I

She's on her way.

I fucked it up.

I fucked it up, and it was all down to that free case of beer.

We drank that whole thing between us - me and Bob. About half of it during the club, and then the other half back at the hotel - with our two thousand dollars spread out on the floor in front of us.

Ray hadn't seemed that impressed when we'd gone to get the second half of it from him.

"That was... unusual," he said.

But we told him that's just what we do.

"Some people like it and some people don't," I said.

"I'm sorry?"

"That's our style," I said. "As far as we're concerned people can take it or leave it."

"What?"

I took a deep breath. I felt pretty sure he was a gun-in-the-drawer-type guy.

"That's our set," Bob told him. "It's not to everyone's taste, but when people like it..."

"Hmm," Ray said, but he paid us all the same.

We went back out through the club and took the beer, then we looked at the pile of records. We were going to just leave them there, but we decided that would probably cause more trouble than taking them, so we gathered them up.

"Who the fuck is this Michael guy?" I asked Bob as he wove the car slowly about the road, and we looked for a hotel.

"He's a cunt," Bob said. "I thought he was a friend."

"Who is he?"

"Just a guy I know in New York. He plays in a few bands. I took his girlfriend out a couple of times when he was away, but I didn't think he knew. I guess he must have found out."

"So this whole thing is about that?"

"I guess so."

"Fuck..." I said. "Still, I'll bet he didn't know what we were getting paid tonight."

"I'll fucking bet he didn't," Bob laughed.

So we drank the rest of the beer back at the hotel, and we got drunk enough not to realise we had nothing left to try now to get this fucking record made. And then, when Bob had gone back to his own room, I did a quick calculation on the time and phoned the wife.

It was a big fucking mistake. I was too drunk and to pleased with myself for having just pulled off what we'd pulled off, and I started going on about how well we were doing.

"You wouldn't believe it," I told her. "They like our ideas so much out here they've started paying us to DJ. Take a guess at how much we made tonight."

"For what?"

"For playing a few records. Five hours work – if you can call it work."

"How much?"

"Two thousand dollars. Two thousand fucking dollars."

She let out a wee scream.

"That's fucking magic, Peacock," she said. "So how soon can you fly me over?"

I put my head in my hands.

"I... I'll look into it, hen," I told her. "I'll sort it out tomorrow."

She was over the fucking moon. I couldn't fucking calm her down.

"I'll give you a wee phone tomorrow when I know what's happening," I told her. "You take it easy now, hen."

Then I hung up, and wept.

★

We were quite a sight at breakfast the next morning, me and the wee man, with our bloodshot eyes and our thumping fucking headaches. And what a fucking breakfast it was. We were sharing a pot of microbiotic twig tea, and eating wholemeal pancakes in some fucking hippy place where it was all roots and shoots.

"I can't fucking believe it," I said to Bob. "There's no fucking stopping her. I can't believe I fucked-up like that."

"We're at a dead end anyway," Bob said. "What are we going to do now? We're all out of leads."

He took a drink of the tea and winced.

"There's only one thing we can do," I told him. "We're going to have to find someone ourselves. Hire someone. We've got the fucking money now."

"I guess so."

"How hard can it be?"

Bob shrugged.

No harder than getting through that breakfast, that was for sure. We fucking struggled with that. And we didn't feel any healthier for it afterwards either.

"Should we look for someone here?" I asked Bob.

He screwed his face up.

"There's a lot more on offer down the coast," he said.

"Where should we go then?" I asked him.

"There's only one place," he said. "LA."

And that was that.

"*Look* at it," I said to Bob. "Jesus *Christ*."

We were at the airport; Los Angeles International Airport. We'd been there for three fucking hours, waiting. Still, it was a spectacular place. It should have been space shuttles that were flying out of there, rather than planes. It looked like a fucking futuristic city.

All the same, the "it" I was drawing Bob's attention to wasn't any feature of the airport – we'd already been there long enough to study all that. The "it" in question was the honourable Mrs Johnson – the fucking wife; teetering out through baggage control on her four-inch heels, carrying more stuff than I thought we owned, and smashed on the free drink from the plane.

"Give me a hand here, Peacock," she shouted, dropping everything.

Bob hurried forward and picked up a couple of her bags.

"Look at the state of my hair," she said. "I had it done before I left. It was lovely. All nice and high. Look at it now. It's *collapsed*. And I fell asleep on this side of it on the plane. What do I look like? I could do with a loan of your hairnet," she said to Bob. "Hello, by the way. You must be the wee madman."

"Evil," I told her. "Evil Bob."

"Hello Evil Bob," she said. "I'm Beverley. Call me Bev. You're right, Peacock. He does look like someone. Someone famous. What a fucking flight that was. I left the house eighteen hours ago. Then it's delayed by three hours. Have you been here long?"

"Aye," I told her. "Three hours."

I picked up two of her bags, and we made our way out to the car.

She gasped when we got outside.

"My God," she said. "It's roasting, Peacock. You should see it back in Glasgow. It *snowed* on Wednesday. It's fucking freezing there. Oh, but this is glorious. You must have been having a great time here. Where's your suntan, Peacock? You're still as white as me. What have you been *doing*?"

"We've been working," I told her. "Besides, we just got here. It hasn't been like this everywhere."

"I'm knackered," she said. "How far are we from the hotel, Peacock? I'm going to have to go to bed when we get there."

"It'll take us about forty minutes," I told her, and we jammed her into the back seat, along with most of her bags. There wasn't room for most of her bags in the boot, and it wasn't a small boot either. There had been room for *me* in there, for fuck sake. But there wasn't room for most of Bev's bags.

"What the fuck have you got in there?" I asked her.

"Just my stuff," she said, and she pushed about amongst it all, trying to make a space for herself to sit in.

Once we got moving she'd somehow managed to clear enough room to poke her head forward into the front, between me and Bob's seats, and she was off again.

"Is it the guy who plays Frazier?" she asked us.

"What?"

"You know, on the telly. The show about the psychiatrist. Is it the guy who plays him?"

"Where?"

"That he *looks* like. Is that who the wee madman looks like?"

"I fucking hope not," Bob said.

"You do a bit though. A thinner version. With hair."

"And a different face," I said.

"He does a bit though."

"Nah," I told her. "It's someone else."

A couple of minutes later she was snoring. Snoring loudly. It didn't sound too pleasant, but I told Bob to enjoy it.

"This might be the only break we get," I said.

And we were in luck. It lasted pretty much all the way back to the hotel - with just one break when she suddenly appeared between our seats again, and stared at herself in the mirror.

"My *God*," she said. "Look at the state of me."

And then she was asleep again.

At the hotel she groaned all the way up to the room, half-asleep with her hangover starting to kick in, and I put her into bed and turned the air-conditioning on.

Then I went out to sit at the edge of the pool with Bob. To relax and get some rest before the evening.

★

We'd got a lot of things started since we arrived in LA, me and Bob. We'd found a few people and worked a few things out, and it hadn't been hard. Things were fucking easy in LA. I kept telling Bob we should have come straight there in the first place. There was just so much going on, so many people trying to get things done. And there were so many people who'd come there expecting to become stars, with all different kinds of talents, that you could easily find someone who could do just whatever you needed. Someone who hadn't become a star yet – and needed any kind of work they could get – just for the money.

There were hundreds of people always looking for something to do, so me and Bob had found our first guy pretty easily. All we'd had to do was look up the back of a newspaper, and to be honest we didn't even really have to go that far. There were things hanging off lamp-posts, and on bins and on newspaper dispensers, saying, "I can do this. Do you need me?"

Things with perforated tickets on the bottom that you could tear off, with their name and phone number on it.

But we'd put a bit of effort in, and found our guy up the back of a newspaper. Or a free arts magazine.

It said something like – "Turn your idea into a hit." Something fucking daft like that. But we gave the number a phone and went along to the place.

It was just one guy in a wee room with a lot of computers and machines. It didn't look like he'd been there long, everything seemed pretty new.

"So what are you looking to do, guys?" he asked us. "Are you a band?"

69

"Do we look like a band?" I said.

"What?"

"Do we..."

"We're not a band," Bob told him. "We've got an idea we want to make into a record."

"Alright."

"There's a well-known song we want to turn into a dance record."

"Uh-huh. We can do that. What's the song?"

"We can't tell you just now," I said.

"What?"

"We're..."

"We don't want anyone else to get hold of the idea yet," Bob told him.

"Uh-huh. Okay. Now," he said, "do you guys have the individual passes on DAT?"

"Do we have what?"

"Do you have each of the tracks individually, from the masters? Is this something the original artists are involved with, or is it something you're working on yourselves?"

"It's our own idea," Bob said.

"And you don't have the tracks individually?"

"All we have is the idea, pal."

"I'm sorry?"

"All we've got..."

"We've got the original record and the idea," Bob said. "That's all."

"Fine. That's not a problem. So there's two ways we can do this. The first way is to take the original record as it is, then add the sounds you want. I can't say how well that would work without knowing what the record is, but it would be the cheapest way. If you just want the track for yourselves, to play in a few clubs I'd guess that's the way to do it. But if you wanted to do more with it, then you'd have trouble. If you couldn't get permission from the artist and the label then you couldn't put it out."

"What's the other way?" Bob asked.

"The other way is more expensive. What you'd do is re-record the track from scratch, then add what you want to add."

"How the fuck would we do that?" I asked him.

He looked at me.

"How would..."

"Neither of us is musical guys," Bob said. "How would we go about that?"

The guy smiled.

"You'd get other people to do it for you," he said. "We couldn't do that here, but I can put you in touch with people who can, and then you'd bring your individual tracks back here and we'd put it together however you want, adding whatever beats you need. You don't have to let them in on your idea at the other studio either," he said. "As far as they're concerned you're making a cover version, that's all. So they won't steal your hit."

He smiled again and then gave us an address, a name and a phone number.

"They do a good job there," he said. "They'll find you good players and they'll charge you reasonable rates. Just tell them you need a DAT of each track individually when you're finished. Here, I'll write that down for you too."

He took the piece of paper back and scribbled on it again. Then he shook our hands.

"Where are you from?" he asked me as we were leaving.

"Scotland," I said.

"Excuse me?"

"Scotland," Bob told him.

"Really? That's fantastic. I love your accent. I really do."

"Cheers, pal," I said.

I don't suppose I have to tell you what he said in reply.

III

Out by the pool me and Bob took it easy, trying to get a bit of sleep on the sunloungers. We were going into the studio that night, and it was going to be a long one. 9pm till 9am. We'd managed to get it a lot cheaper during those hours, and I was just hoping it fucking worked out. Even at those night-time prices we could still only afford this one shot.

We'd told the guy there the song we wanted recorded, and he said he could find the people to play it, no problem.

"Find someone who can really sing it," I told him. "We don't want any fucking lady-boy. We want someone who can sing it like Glen."

He told me not to worry, he knew just the guy.

"You won't be disappointed," he said, and then he'd shown us round the place and we'd set the date.

Dozing out there on the sunlounger I kept dreaming it was all going wrong. In one dream none of the musicians had ever heard the song and we couldn't find a recording of it. I was trying to tell them how to play it, but each time I spoke they just said,

"What?" or "Sorry?"

Even in fucking dreams...

Then I had this one where everything was going good. It sounded great. But while we were listening to it Glen himself burst into the room. He'd heard about what we were up to and he wasn't happy about it.

"Peacock!" he shouted as he came tearing in. "Peacock!"

I woke up from that one, but the shouting carried on.

"Peacock!"

"Peacock!"

I tried to work out where the fuck I was, and, still dozing, I looked up, up to where the shouting seemed to be coming from. And all I could see was a great fucking sheet of water coming down towards me. It hit me with a real fucking thump, and I leapt up out of the chair, fucking drenched.

I could hear the wife cackling away up there.

"Peacock you lazy bastard," she shouted. "Time to wake up.

This is Hollywood. No one ever sleeps in Hollywood."

"You stupid cow," I shouted back.

Bob was laughing too, but not for long. While I was shaking myself off another sheet came down and landed on him.

"Fuck..." he spluttered, and shook himself like a dog.

We ran into the hotel and got into the lift, but by the time we'd got to the room she'd locked herself in the bathroom.

"Get out of there," I shouted, and she cackled like a mad fucking witch, but she wouldn't unlock the door.

"Leave me alone," she shouted back.

So Bob went off to his room to get changed, and I took off my wet stuff.

"I need a towel," I shouted to her then. "Open the fucking door."

"No."

"Come on, I'm fucking soaking."

I heard some stuff going on in there and then I heard the lock click, but the door didn't open.

I pushed it slowly and went in. She was standing over at the bath with the shower-head in her hand. She'd taken it off the wall and had one hand on the tap.

"Stay away," she said. "Take your towel and get out. I'm not scared to use this thing."

"You're crazy," I told her and grabbed a towel.

"Stay back," she said, but she turned it on anyway. The spray hit my back and I ran out.

"You're a fucking mad woman," I shouted, and she started cackling again. I could hear her struggling to get the shower-head back on the wall and then she came through.

"What's the fucking idea?" I asked her. "You're insane."

"Ah, but you love me all the same," she said. "Don't you, Peacock?"

She started fucking up my hair while I was drying myself.

"Ah, my wee Peacock," she said. And she planted these big daft kisses on my face, pulling my head about.

"He loves his Bev, don't you Peacock? Wee Peacock."

"Get off," I told her, but I didn't have to. She'd seen herself in the mirror and she was already on her way over there for a closer look.

"Jesus Christ," she said. "Look at the state of my fucking hair. It's a disaster. Here I am in Hollywood, and look at my hair. It cost me a fucking fortune too. Fifty quid. Fifty quid and I look like a fucking trollop."

She started pulling at bits of it, while I found myself a clean shirt and vest, and another pair of shorts.

"What have you got planned for us for this evening anyway?" she asked me. "Can we go to see some of the film studios? I want to see that street where they have all the stars in the pavement. But I read they do tours of the studios. What do you want to do first?"

"Me and the wee man are working," I said. "I told you, we're not on fucking holiday."

"What are you doing?" she asked.

"We're going to oversee the first part of the recording."

"Oversee? What the fuck do you know about overseeing, Peacock? Still, it might be interesting. Have they recorded the music for any films in that studio?"

"How the fuck would I know?"

"I'll bet they have. Oh, it's exciting – just thinking about what might have been made there. And then tomorrow we can go and see the street with the stars in the pavement, and find out about one of those tours. I can hardly wait. I'm going to love it here, Peacock. It's going to be great."

"Fucking hell..." I muttered.

IV

At five to nine the three of us arrived at the studio in a taxi. Bev wanted to know why we were in a normal taxi and not a fucking limousine. She wouldn't shut up about it.

"What kind of people are you working for?" she asked us.

"This is *Hollywood*. Trust *you*, Peacock, to end up working for a company that sends you about in a normal taxi. This isn't what I expected at all. I thought we'd have a TV in here, long leather sofas. A wee fridge full of champagne - and all the stuff we needed to make cocktails."

She had a fucking cocktail with her anyway. Something they'd made for her in the place we'd had dinner. Something called a Humphrey-fucking-Bogart. She couldn't get over the name of it. It looked just like any other cocktail she'd ever had, a strange neon blue colour. It probably had the same stuff in it too. But she loved it cause it was called a Humphrey Bogart, and she'd wanted to take one to the studio with her, so I'd had to pay for the fucking glass.

"Excuse me," she said to the driver on the way there. "Could you slow down on the corners, I don't want to spill my drink."

"There's no drinking allowed in here, lady," he told her.

She looked at me.

She shook her head.

Then she started banging on about us being in a normal taxi again.

When we finally got to the studio she slammed the car door shut and the end of the fucking ridiculous feather-boa she was wearing got caught inside. Then the guy started driving away.

She had to run after him, wobbling on the heels, holding the Humphrey Bogart up high in one hand, and shouting, "Slow down. Stop. Slow down. Help me, Peacock. Stop him. Stop."

"What the fuck are you wearing that for anyway?" I asked her, after he'd released the thing, and she'd come staggering back along.

"I didn't think we'd be in a fucking taxi," she said. "I thought we'd be working for people with a bit more *class*. But I should have known. I should have known what sort of thing you'd be involved with."

The feather-boa was pink. The top she had on was green and orange. Her trousers were brown. She was one to be talking about class.

"If we'd come in a limousine they'd have fucking thrown you out for looking like that," I told her, and she drew me a look as we went inside.

Our guy Gerry, who owned the place, was there waiting for us, and he took us through into the lounge area. Bev latched onto him like a fucking limpet and started banging on, in great detail, about the limousine our company had sent us there in.

"It was much bigger then we needed," she laughed. "But who's complaining? I mixed this wee drink for myself in there too. I'm sure they won't mind that I took the glass. Do you think they'll mind?"

"What the fuck are you playing at?" I whispered to her when he went off to check something.

"You don't want him to know what kind of outfit you're really working for," she said. "Otherwise he'll treat you like shit."

"He probably saw us arriving in the fucking taxi," I told her. "All the fucking commotion you caused out there was bound to attract his attention."

"Fuck off, Peacock..." she said.

When he came back Bob asked him if the musicians had arrived yet, and he told us the drummer was just setting up.

"The piano player and the guitarist are here," he said. "And the bass player – if you can call a bass player a musician. We're just waiting on the singer and the guy who's going to do the string samples – then we'll mic everything up and we'll be ready to go. Come on through to the control room."

He held the door open for us and introduced us to another guy in there.

"Spike is my tape opp," he said. "If you need anything you just ask him. He'll be more than happy to get it for you. Anything at all. Right, Spike?"

Spike nodded.

There was a big window in there that looked into another room, and in the other room we could see the drummer setting up, and the rest of them knocking about on their instruments.

Gerry pressed a button on a desk that was just a fucking mass of buttons.

"Guys," he said. "Take a minute and come through to meet the guys who are paying you tonight."

So they all put down what they were doing and came through. Bev pushed to the front and lifted one hand up high for some kind of fucking ridiculous society handshake, still sipping from the cocktail.

All four of them looked pretty bemused, but they shook her hand all the same.

"Guys," Gerry said. "This is Beverley. And these two fellows are Bob and Peacock."

We shook hands with them too.

"Rob on drums, Eddy on guitar, Marshall on piano and Mark on bass," Gerry said. "These guys are the best there are."

We knew he was talking shite, cause we knew what we were paying them to stay up all night. But we pretended anyway.

"It's just a shame you're not getting to play a better song," Bev said to them, and they laughed.

"What the fuck are you talking about?" I asked her. "You like the song."

"I like it, Peacock," she said. "But it'll be hard going for them having to listen to it all night. I *know*. I have to do it often enough when you're in one of your moods."

"What kind of music do you like?" the drummer asked her.

"Oh, older stuff," she said, her voice softening. "I like singers with a bit of class. Dean Martin, Tony Bennet. Frank."

"That's good stuff," the drummer said.

Then they went back to their room again.

"*Glen* has class," I told her. "Glen has plenty of fucking class."

"*Relax*, Peacock," she said. "Relax. You're fucking obsessed. Spike..."

The assistant guy looked up.

"I wonder," she said. "Do you think you could make me another cocktail?"

"Sure," he said. "I can do that. What do you want in it?"

"Oh, I don't mind," she told him. "Just so long as it tastes nice."

He went off with her empty glass, and while he was gone the string guy arrived.

"Alright," Gerry said. "We're just waiting for the singer now. I'll start setting the mics up, and when he gets here we'll be ready to go."

V

I very nearly shat myself. I thought it was him.

I turned to Bob and he was staring too.

Bev didn't give a fuck, of course. She was nattering on to Spike about the cocktail he'd brought her.

"It's so *smooth*," she was saying. "Delicious."

But I just stared with my mouth open.

"Hi guys," he said. "I'm Jack. Is Gerry around?"

"Through there," Bob told him.

He nodded.

"What should I call you guys?"

"Bob," Bob said. "And this is Peacock."

We shook his hand, and even though I knew it wasn't him I felt fucking star-struck. I wasn't even able to speak to the cunt. I just stared.

He had Glen's square jaw, Glen's hair from the 70's. He was even wearing Glen's fucking clothes.

He was wearing a denim jacket that was all styled up like a cowboy shirt, with a pattern on the shoulders and the pockets and the cuffs. A flared pair of denims and cowboy boots. He even had the fucking side-burns.

When I thought about it, I knew even Glen wouldn't look like that now – cause this guy was the same age now as Glen was back then. But if you'd met the two of them together – Glen the way he is now, and this guy – you'd have gone for this guy as being

78

the real thing.

"Did you see that?" I asked Bev, when he'd gone through to the other room.

"What?" she said. "Was that the singer getting here?"

"Aye. Did you see him?"

"He looked like a big fucking jessy," she said.

"Did he fuck," I whispered. "He looked exactly like *Glen*."

"That's what I mean, Peacock. You're obsessed, you know. *Obsessed*."

I gave up on her. I turned to Bob.

"How about that?" I asked him.

"That freaked me out," he said. "That was fucking uncanny."

It got more uncanny too. When Gerry came back through, he got them all to play their instruments one at a time, while he moved some of those buttons on the desk. And when it came to the singer's turn he sounded exactly like him too. Probably more than he looked like him.

I stared at Bob and Bob stared at me. Bev slurped her cocktail.

"Alright," Gerry said. "Give me something all together, guys. Anything at all."

They started banging around on all different songs, and then they stopped, laughing.

"Okay," one of them said. You could hear them speaking in our room, but only very faintly, through the speakers.

"How about this, Beverley," one of them shouted, and they started playing again, joining in one at a time as the tune went on. Then the singer started singing, 'Strangers in the Night.' That fucking woke her up. She got up out of her chair and started dancing around – a slow dance, holding her cocktail up in the air and swaying from side to side, twirling her fucking feather-boa.

The guy sounded exactly like one of those old singers now, nothing like Glen at all, and she was in her fucking element. When they finished that song they started playing 'That's Amore', and she ran through to the other room, and started dancing in there. We could see her through the window, waltzing about on her own, then, at the instrumental, the singer partnered her, and they waltzed about together, her holding the cocktail up high above his shoulder.

I could hear she was talking in there when the song finished, but I couldn't hear what she was saying. We didn't have to wait long to find out what it had been about though. The band soon started up again, and this time she was singing.

'Sugar Town.'

She fucking loves that song. It drives me fucking mental, listening to it blasting at home, with her singing along badly.

She wasn't doing any better here either. It didn't sound too good. Luckily it's not too long a song, so it was soon over.

"Alright," Gerry said then, laughing and pressing his button down so's they could all hear him talking through there. "That's me ready to go, guys. We're up and running."

The drummer stuck a thumb up, and then they all talked a bit more. I could hear Bev laughing, and the singer spoke into the microphone.

"Gerry," he said. "Let's roll the tapes and we'll put this down first, just to help everyone loosen up."

"Fine," Gerry said, and nodded to Spike.

It took me a bit to catch on - it took me till they were playing again. Then I fucking got it.

"Aww, Jesus Christ," I said to Bob.

Three minutes later we had Bev singing 'Sugar Town' for fucking posterity. She kept waving to me through the glass while she was doing it, then closing her eyes to presumably put what she thought was some feeling into it. At each chorus she'd lift her glass *and* close her eyes - "Shoo-shoo-*shoo*." And up it would come.

It was fucking brutal. And she didn't even sing it as well as she had the first time. The whole thing was pretty ropey really. But she was fucking thrilled when she came back through. Chuffed to bits. Spike put it onto a CD for her and then went to get her another cocktail. She was practically floating about the room.

"Alright, guys," Gerry said, with his finger on his button again. "Let's have a shot at what we're here for."

And they ran through 'Rhinestone Cowboy' for the first time.

To be honest it was a long night after that, and most of it was pretty boring. The first time they ran through the song was fucking amazing, just because it sounded so good. It sounded fucking incredible. I couldn't believe they were all just through there playing it like that, and I got a bit fucking emotional, thinking that's what it must have been like to be there on the night Glen originally recorded it.

But after they'd played it another three or four times, they all started packing up their instruments, and they got ready to go home.

I thought it was all over then. I thought we were nearly finished, and I was amazed.

"This is going to cost us a lot less than we thought," I said to Bob, but I was fucking wrong.

When the musicians had gone we listened to the recordings with Gerry, and chose the best one – and after that it just seemed to go on and on.

And on.

He spent fucking hours listening to each instrument on its own, turning and twisting the nobs. Then he spent more hours listening to them all together – turning and twisting again.

Bev went back to the hotel sometime around then.

"I can't take any more of this, Peacock," she said. "It's driving me daft."

And making sure that everyone else could hear she said,

"Is the limousine coming back for us or should I get a taxi."

"You should get a taxi," I told her.

So Spike went and phoned for one.

When it turned up I went out with her. Not out of any desire to be with her – I just needed to get away from the music, and all that fucking incessant twisting.

"What room are we in, Peacock?" she asked.

"Two fifteen."

"What street are we on?"

"Sunset Boulevard."

She climbed into the taxi, struggling not to spill a drop of her latest cocktail. And as the guy pulled off I saw her leaning forward, and heard her shouting at him to put her CD in the stereo.

Poor fucking cunt.

VI

We came out of the studio straight into the LA rush hour, me and the wee man. The daylight hurt my eyes, and we were a bit drunk by then too.

The last part of the operation had been the most tedious of them all. Gerry had been recording each instrument separately onto a tape for us, and in the end we'd just had to leave him to it, and go and sit in the lounge.

It was alright in there. There was a TV and armchairs, and – most importantly – you couldn't hear any music coming from the studio. We had Spike bring us a few beers in there, and we watched some of the crap they put on TV in the middle of the night. Then a bit later Bob found a channel showing a recording of an old American football game – so we watched that for a while.

It's a fucking strange game, American football. In a way it's a lot like their TV shows; as soon as it starts to get going they stop it. You can understand it a bit more with the TV programmes, cause they want to show you as many adverts as possible. But fuck knows what it is with the football. Mind you, it's a bit like the country itself; you drive for a thousand miles and see fuck-all. Then – suddenly – you see something unbelievable, something totally fucking spectacular. You get all excited, and then it's gone. And it's another thousand miles of fuck-all again.

While we were watching the TV in there I started hatching the idea that they'd had to invent adverts by necessity, cause they couldn't take too much of anything at once, and they needed a reason to keep stopping the programmes. Maybe they should have gone the whole way, I thought, and just made it exactly like the country - just have a blank screen and silence for the length of time the adverts took up. That would be more fucking like it.

Still, I made an effort to understand the game. I kept asking Bob questions about it, and trying to grasp it.

He didn't like me calling it American football though.

"What the fuck is with that, Peacock?" he kept saying. "Why do you call it that. It's football. Just football. No American - just fucking football."

"It's not football to me, son," I told him. "Anyway, they fucking carry the ball most of the time. Feet hardly come into it. It's more like fucking rugby. Except for the armour."

"When you're here, Peacock," he said, "call it football."

"I can't, son. This isn't football. This is American football. Football's a great game. This is all fucked-up."

"Fine," he said. "Fine. American football." And he started trying to explain what I'd asked him about originally, but I still didn't have much of an understanding of the game when it finished.

So we drank some more and watched some more crap, and finally Gerry came to tell us he was done.

"It's been a long night, guys," he said.

"You're not wrong, son," I told him, and he took us into his office.

We gave him a thousand dollars there and he gave us a tape.

"You've got the full song on there first, guys," he said. "Then a test tone, and all the individual tracks are after that. I've written it all on the case, and I've burned you a CD of the full song too, so you can listen to it at home."

He gave us that and we shook hands.

"I think you'll be happy with it," he told us. "It sounds good."

"Cheers, son," I said, and we left.

Taking a taxi in their rush hour was a bit like watching their football and their TV programmes. Something would happen for a few minutes and then nothing; we'd just be sitting there again. And it was a lot more expensive than watching their sports or their TV.

"What did you think of that?" Bob asked me, as we sat stranded again.

"It almost drove me mental," I told him, and he laughed.

"It was good while the musicians were there though," he said. "That was alright. It might be an okay life, being one of those guys."

"Maybe," I said. "But I wouldn't want to be Gerry. That would fucking kill me."

We'd taken some beers away with us, and Bob opened them up - but the driver was way ahead of us.

"You no drink in here," he shouted. "No allowed."

"Aww, come on, pal," I shouted back. "We've been working all night."

"What?"

"We've been working all night."

"I no hear you. What you say?"

"Aye, alright - alright, pal. We'll keep them."

"What?"

"Don't worry," Bob said. "We'll keep them. We'll take them back to the hotel."

"Okay. Okay," he said.

And he started driving again. For about fifteen seconds. Then we came to another stop.

It got so that I couldn't bear to look at the meter. We were almost at the point where it would have been cheaper to hire a limousine. But when we got close to the hotel Bob leant over and whispered to me.

"Take a drink," he said.

"What?"

"Take a drink from your bottle. Go on."

So I did. And while I was drinking he put his thumb over the top of his and started shaking it.

"Keep drinking," he told me, and he pulled his thumb back so that his started spraying about.

The driver slammed the breaks on.

"You get out," he shouted, and Bob put his mouth over the spray and started drinking too. "You get out of my car. Look at the mess you make. You get out. You both get out."

"But we're almost there," Bob pleaded. "It's only another few blocks. Please. We'll stop drinking."

Then came the gun.

"You get out," he screamed. "You get out my car. Lunatics. Get out."

"Go," Bob said, and we got out and ran. Then we stopped.

Bob was cracking himself up.

"How about that?" he asked me, panting and laughing. "How about that, Peacock? Eh? That fare would have sent his kids to college."

"You're a genius," I told him.

"I impress *me* sometimes," he said, and he started cracking up again.

"Still," I told him. "You've wasted a perfectly good bottle of beer there, son."

He held it up and looked at it sadly.

"There is that," he said. "There is that."

Bev was still sleeping when I got back to the room. She was snoring away in there, and it was as dark as night-time with the curtains closed, so I felt around for my CD player and got into bed beside her.

I was fucking knackered, but I put the headphones on anyway and had a listen to the CD Gerry had made. Then I had a listen to Glen's original. Glen's still had that extra magic, but ours sounded good. Ours sounded alright.

Bev started to move around a bit then, so I turned the volume down and watched her till she was settled again. Unfortunately though, Glen's CD had run on from 'Rhinestone Cowboy' to 'Marie' by then, and as Bev snuggled into the pillow I started to feel glad she was there.

It always fucking gets to me, that song. Especially when I've had a few drinks. And before I lay down I kissed her on the forehead.

"Peacock?" she muttered.

"Aye, hen," I said. "Go back to sleep. It's still early."

"Alright," she said.

I won't tell you what I said to her then, and I fucking hope she never heard me either. That bastard song. It'll be the fucking end of me one of these days...

VII

It's totally mental when you think about it. In New York, Bob says, there are thousands of places where we could have got all this done. I could have flown straight there, met him at home, and got the thing made in no time. But instead, because he took a girl out to dinner once or twice, we've travelled fuck-knows how many hundreds of miles, and been through fuck-knows what.

Still, if we'd tried to do things that way we'd never have made the money we made from our wee DJing job, to pay for the fucking thing in the first place. And more importantly we wouldn't be looking at this chance of a record deal we're looking at now, if we can sort ourselves out. So I suppose we have the wee man's romantic skills to thank for everything.

It works both ways.

You should have seen our guy's face when we took him the tapes and played him the song. We didn't tell him what it was before we played it – we just sparked it up, and you should have fucking seen him.

To begin with his face just froze, then the eyes went wide. And by the time he looked up from his desk he had a huge fucking grin on.

"Fuck," he said, shaking his head. Then he was up on his feet.

"Guys," he said, "this is fucking genius." He started laughing and shaking his fists.

"Fuck," he said again. "I love it. *Love* it."

He was so excited he wanted to get to work on it straight away, but we had find out how much it was going to cost us first, cause we knew we didn't have too much money left.

"How much would you want?" Bob asked him, and it just about killed us when he told us the price. It was way more than what we had left, and we knew we'd fucked-up, cause he had the idea for the song now, and if we didn't get it done there, there was nothing to stop him doing the same thing himself.

"How much can you guys stretch to?" he asked us, when we told him we couldn't afford it, and we let him know. We were pretty much down to five hundred dollars. He'd asked for two thousand.

He looked down at his desk.

"This is hard," he said. "I really think this could work. And on top of that, I know a guy in DC who'd put this out if you took it to him. He's got a label, and he'd kill for this. But..."

He rewound the tape and started playing it again. The grin came back.

"You really think he'd put it out?" Bob asked.

"I know he would," the guy said. "He'd love it."

He picked up a pen from the desk and played around with it.

"I'll tell you what," he said. "Maybe I could do this for a bit less. Maybe I could manage it for fifteen hundred. How does that sound? Could you guys raise that kind of money? I'll do it for fifteen hundred if you can cut me in for ten per cent of whatever you make on the record."

So we told him we'd see what we could do. It sounded good, but we knew we'd have to raise enough to get us to DC too. Five hundred was all we had, and that wasn't even enough to fly me and Bev home from there – so we knew we'd have to fucking go for it. It was the only way. And I knew that if we could get it done and get to DC, everything else would sort itself out.

All we needed was a plan.

★

"You wouldn't have believed it, Peacock," Bev said. She was just back from her film studio tour, and she wouldn't stop banging on about it. "I can't even explain properly how it felt," she said. "Just to stand on the same spot where all those films were made. It was..."

We'd taken her up to the street with the stars on it before we'd gone to see our guy, and when we left her she'd gone off on this thing. It had cost a fucking fortune, but I couldn't let her know that was a problem. She still thought we were with some company.

"There was something the tour guide said to us," she told me. "He said one reason film stars are called stars is because by the time you see them on the screen they're already gone. And with the real stars, the legends, you're watching them after they've been dead for years and years. Still shining. Just like the stars in the sky do. I'd never thought of that before, Peacock. I just love it here. I never want to leave."

"We might be leaving soon," I told her. "Me and Bob have to take this thing to Washington when it's done."

"Aww, *Pea*cock," she said. "But I only just got here."

"I know, hen. But I told you before you came, we're here to work. It's not a holiday."

"Can I stay then? Can I fly back home from here later on? After you've gone."

"We'll see," I told her. "We'll see how the money is. Forget that just now though, I'm fucking starving. Let's go and get the wee man and we'll find something to eat."

She'd found a place earlier in the day that she was desperate to go to. Somewhere called Oscars or something, where they had film stills on the wall, and a fucking man-sized Oscar trophy in the corner. It was tacky, but she loved it, and she started banging on to Bob about the reason why film stars are called stars.

I had to give the wee man credit – he managed to sound a lot more interested in her tour than I'd been able to. That whole side of the town was starting to get to me. The street with the stars on it had just about driven me mental, and in here the menu was full of stuff like Hollywood Burgers, and Brando Steaks.

I couldn't really listen to Bev going on about it anymore, but the wee man was doing alright. He was doing fine.

"Why do they call you *Evil* Bob?" Bev asked him, and he grinned.

"Oh, he can be bad," I told her.

"I've got a worm inside me," he said.

"A what?"

"A worm. It makes me do things. I can't get rid of it."

"Yuck," Bev said. "That's disgusting, Bob. Suddenly I don't feel so hungry anymore."

"I told you he could be bad," I said, and Bob laughed.

But she soon got over it, when her Sinatra Salad arrived – and she was off again, nudging me and whispering that she thought the two guys opposite us were film directors, talking about their latest films.

"It's just so exciting here," she said. "Don't you just love it, Bob? It'll break my heart to have to leave. I'll tell you what you should do. You should stop wearing that hairnet, and then you might get mistaken for the guy you look like. Someone might put you in a film by accident, and then we could all live here on your money forever."

"What makes you think he'd share it with us?" I asked her.

"He'd have to," she said. "We'd be the only people who knew who he really was. We'd know he was really just the wee madman. And if he didn't pay us we could let the cat out of the bag."

"You've got it all figured out, eh Bev?"

"Of course I have," she said. "And he'd get me into that film too, wouldn't you, Bob? Just a wee part, nothing too fancy. Just so's you could see me up there even though I'd be gone."

Bob laughed, and then he looked down at his Chaplin

Chicken Stir-Fry.

"It's a good plan," he said. "But I could never do that kind of work, Bev. They're a different kind of people altogether, actors. Same as those guys we were working with the other night. It's a whole other thing, creating."

"How is it?" Bev asked him.

"It just is," Bob said. "Before I left New York I was at a comedy club watching this guy, and he was just awesome. Someone shouted something at him, some kind of abuse - and he came straight back at them - instantly. And then *he* started laughing at what he'd said. "Where the fuck did that come from?" he asked us. And all through the act you could see these things occurring to him just before he said them, and you could see him struggling not to laugh. That's how it works. I'm always thinking that very same thing - "Where the fuck did that come from?" But it's different with me. I'm on the other side of the coin. The things that occur to me are destructive things. Nasty ideas. It's this worm. It just fucking *crawls* in there..."

"You don't seem *that* nasty to me," Bev said.

"Oh, I can be," Bob told her. "I can be..."

And he got stuck back into the stir-fry.

★

Before we left there he gave her a wee demonstration. She'd kept asking him about his worm all through the rest of the meal, and telling him he didn't seem that evil to her - till I think it finally got on his nerves.

So in the end he stood up and told her he'd show her something. Then he just walked out of the place.

For a while we sat there wondering if that was it, if that was his demonstration - just leaving us there to wait for him while he never came back. But soon he reappeared at the window, waving in at us, and he was holding a chain.

"What's he got that for?" Bev asked me, in a bit of a panic. "What's he going to do, Peacock?"

But I told her I'd no idea. "He's a fucking live wire, hen," I said.

She tried to signal to him to come back inside, but he was grinning his mad grin. He waved to us again and then started crossing the road.

"I shouldn't have encouraged him," she said. "Should I? Do you think it's my fault? What's that worm he keeps going on about anyway? Has he told you about that before?"

"He's mentioned it," I said.

"Well what is it?"

"I don't know. I don't ask him. I just let him bang on about it."

"I should have kept my mouth shut," she said.

But soon the wee man was back in the restaurant again, sitting at the table with us.

When he'd got across the road all he'd done with his chain was wrap it around a pole, and then slip it through the wheel of a motorbike that was sitting there, and fasten it up.

He was in fucking stitches when he came back to the table, though.

"That's awful, Bob," Bev said to him, and he knocked the key for the chain against his glass.

"How much did that cost you?" I asked him.

"Nothing," he said. "I stole it. Now all we have to do is wait."

To be honest I didn't really want to wait in there any longer. That big Oscar thing was starting to disturb me, and the whole place was grinding me down. But it turned out we didn't have to wait too long. Soon Bob started tapping his key frantically on the table and cracking himself up again.

"Here he comes," he said. "Here he comes." And we watched as a guy in leathers walked towards the bike.

He didn't even notice the chain at first. He just took the bike off its stand and hopped on. It wasn't till he started trying to roll forward that he realised it was stuck.

"Strike one," Bob shouted, laughing away to himself.

We paid up and got out of there then, and we could hear the guy muttering away to himself across the street.

"Motherfucker!" he shouted at one point, and he kicked the chain.

"Go and unlock it for him," Bev said to Bob, but he wouldn't do it. He held the key out and then let it drop down a drain.

"Jesus," Bev said to him. "You *are* an evil wee shite."

"I told you so," he laughed, looking back at the guy. "And you know what he's thinking right now to himself, don't you?"

"What?"

"He's thinking – *Where the fuck did that come from…*"

VIII

The problem we had later, though, was that the worm appeared to be asleep. He seemed to have worn it out, and we needed its help to come up with a plan. We needed a way to make some fucking money.

Bev had gone to bed not long after we'd come back from dinner, worn out from all the excitement of her tour, and I'd taken the chance to slip through to Bob's room to try and sort something out with him. But we were fucking struggling.

We'd spread all the money out on the bed, and counted it up. It came to five hundred and eighty six dollars, plus some change, and we were just sitting staring at it; stuck.

"All we need is another thousand for the song," I said. "Then enough to get us to Washington. How many days will that take us?"

"Probably five," Bob said. "It's a long fucking way. And we need to renew the lease on the car, that's about to expire."

"What?"

Bob shrugged. "There's only a couple more days on it," he said.

"It's a fucking pity the rumour about us being DJs didn't spread," I told him. "Another night of that and we'd be laughing."

"Another night of that would get us lynched, Peacock. And I'll tell you what else."

"What?"

"Ever since we did that I've been haunted by one of the songs we played. I keep getting this vague picture in my mind of us singing it. I think it must have been one of the songs we did at karaoke."

"Which song?"

"You don't want to know. Remember, we agreed never to talk about it. Just be glad it's in my head and not yours."

He opened the mini-bar and got us a beer each. I thought back over some of the songs we'd played that night and then decided I didn't want to remember. I had the feeling if I thought about it properly it would come back all too easily, and he was right – I was glad it was in his head and not mine.

"Alright," he said as he opened his beer. "Let's get to work, worm. This should wake you up. Come on, we need a plan..."

★

And this is what his worm came up with. Are you ready for it?

Housebreaking.

It was hardly a fucking master-stroke, but then again, it was more than I'd managed. For a long time I'd just sat there drinking from the mini-bar and thinking we were fucked.

Admittedly I hadn't really wanted to get back into any kind of crime. It's like I said; there's not enough money in it anymore. But we didn't have a lot of options, and with it being LA I supposed there would probably be a lot more money in *everything* here than there was anywhere else. So we had the valet guy bring the car round to the front of the hotel and we went out looking.

The worm's original idea had been more specific than just housebreaking. It's first suggestion had been housebreaking in Beverly Hills, so that was where we started out.

It was fucking obvious when we got there though that it was

a no-go. Every house had a sign at the entrance letting you know there were guards and dogs on patrol. Armed guards, and probably armed fucking dogs too. And the signs made it clear that they were perfectly prepared to shoot you on sight; that they would positively relish the chance to take a pop at you. And all of this was presuming you could actually get into the grounds in the first place, which didn't look likely, what with the height of the walls and the strength of the gates.

"Bad worm," Bob said, and slapped his stomach. "Bad worm." And we decided to get out of there and go looking for somewhere a bit more doable.

We kept passing cars on the way down that were crawling along about three miles an hour, with people in the passenger seats pointing torches at maps. It was like a fucking road-rally for kerb-crawlers, and curiosity got the better of me in the end. I had to get Bob to pull up beside one and ask them what it was all about.

It turned out you could buy a map in town telling you which film stars and singers lived in which mansions.

"We'll have to make sure Bev doesn't find out about that," I told Bob as we drove away. "Otherwise we'll be spending a miserable afternoon up here again tomorrow."

"Fucking weird," Bob said, as he swerved out to overtake another one of them, and we headed off towards the less affluent streets.

We had to be careful choosing our area. If the houses were too run down there would be fuck-all worth stealing inside, but it seemed that anyone who had anything at all was protecting it all-out. We got to thinking it might even be a status thing; the more security you had the more the neighbours would think you had to protect. So there might have been fuck-all in a lot of those houses too.

What we were really looking for was some kind of rebel. Someone who'd decided all that show was unnecessary, and stepped out the race. Then we could prove to them that they were wrong, and that it was all necessary. Do them a service, if you like.

But we looked for a long fucking time. We drove through all kinds of neighbourhoods, and we did find some places that we thought could be done, but there was a lot of life going on in them all.

"What the fuck are you doing at home, you freaks!" Bob shouted. "You're living in LA for fuck sake. Get out and *party*."

Finally though, we did find a street that looked pretty dead. Bob drove along slowly and we looked at some houses. Then he stopped.

"What do you think?" he asked me.

"Let's get out and have a look," I said.

We'd decided there was no point in taking anything other than cash. Maybe jewellery at a push. But we didn't want the hassle of trying to sell anything. We didn't know how it went there, and we didn't know anyone who did. So it was bound to be more trouble than it was worth.

"Which one do you think?" I asked Bob, and he walked up and down. There was one place sitting off on its own more than the others, and we decided that was the one. There was less chance of anyone in any of the other houses hearing us trying to get in there and, like Bob said, it looked like the kind of place a weirdo would live in. Someone who kept all their savings under the mattress.

"What does the worm reckon?" I asked him, but he didn't laugh.

"Don't fucking joke about that, Peacock," he said. "It's not a fucking thing of amusement."

He looked pretty rattled, so I apologised to him and said I'd been out of order, just so's we could fucking get on with things.

"Alright," I said. "Forget it. Let's go."

Although it didn't have any of the obvious protection we'd seen everywhere else, it was still pretty secure. Nothing gave way or opened easily.

"You go to the front," Bob said in the end, when we'd tried all the windows at the back of the house. "I'm small enough to get through that one if I break it. You make sure no one's out front and I'll open the door for you when I get through."

So round I went.

He must have broken the window quietly, cause I didn't hear a fucking thing. I was still out there listening for it when I heard a scream from inside the house instead. It came from somewhere near the back, followed by the sound of things falling, and then I could hear someone running towards the front door.

I tried to get away then, but the door burst open almost instantly, and it was the wee man who came tearing out.

"Go," he shouted at me. "Go, go, go."

Then he pushed me and I went flat out on my back. I could see him still running from where I lay on the ground.

"Bob," I shouted at him, but he didn't turn round. He was fucking possessed. He got to the car and started fumbling for his keys, and I noticed that in one hand he was holding what looked like a fucking teapot.

I got up and ran after him.

By the time I got my door open the car was already fucking moving. I had to throw myself in, and if I hadn't got there in time I don't think he'd have waited for me. He looked fucking petrified.

I turned round as we pulled off, to see who was coming after us, but there was no one. The house was still in darkness, and the door was lying open. There was no one anywhere on the street but us.

"What the fuck happened?" I asked him.

"You don't want to know," he said.

"Of course I fucking do. Who screamed?"

"Me."

"*You?*"

"Let's just get out of here," he said, and he cranked up the speed. We screeched round a corner and off that street, and the fucking teapot skidded across the dashboard. I caught it and looked inside.

"Aww fuck..." I said. It was fucking rank. There was a puddle of tea in the bottom that had green mould floating about in it.

"What the fuck did you bring this for?" I asked him.

"I had to bring something," he said. "If I'd come out empty-handed the whole thing would have been a waste of time."

"And this makes it all worthwhile?"

"I guess not," he said.

He wouldn't say anything else about what had happened all the way back to the hotel. In fact, he didn't say anything else at all. He just drove, with that frightened look on his face, a bit too fast. And when we got back to his room he threw open the mini-bar, and grabbed a bottle.

"Help yourself," he told me, and then he lay down on the bed, and covered his eyes with his hand.

There wasn't much left in there. We'd finished off everything except a few miniatures before we'd gone out, but I dug around till I found a whisky, and then I tried to get the wee man talking.

It wasn't fucking easy. Everything came out in bits and pieces, and he kept stopping and covering his face up again, but eventually I managed to piece most of it together.

"You certainly got in without making a sound," I told him, and he said that was the first thing that had surprised him.

"I knocked the window in, and it didn't make a sound when it hit the floor," he said. So he'd lowered himself down onto the sink and let his eyes grow accustomed to the darkness, and when he'd been able to see better it had started to look like the floor was moving.

"I thought it was just the pattern on the tiles at first," he said. "I thought it was some kind of fucked-up illusion. But it didn't smell too good in there, and when I got down onto the floor it *crunched*. It fucking crunched, Peacock, and I could feel it moving."

He looked like he was going to start crying then, and he swallowed hard. And are you ready for this? Are you ready for what he told me? He said the fucking floor had been covered in worms.

"That's when I screamed," he said. "And I just fucking ran. I knocked something over and I grabbed that fucking teapot, but mostly I just needed to get out of there."

"Are you sure they were worms?" I asked him, and he said he was sure.

"But how the fuck does a floor get covered in worms?"

"I don't fucking know," he said. "But they were there. They're everywhere, Peacock. They fucking *follow* me..."

He covered his face up again and I had no idea what to say, so I said fuck-all. I got us another bottle each from the mini-bar and put one into Bob's hand. He took a drink from it and spluttered.

"What the fuck is that, Peacock?" he asked me, and took his hand away from his face. We were down to liqueurs by then. "Oh, Jesus..." he said. "Is this all that's left?"

I nodded.

He took another drink from it and spluttered again.

"This is no good" he said. "We can't drink this, Peacock. This won't do at all. Come on, let's go down to the bar."

But before we went down, he drained the liqueur anyway.

IX

It was a harrowing night. We drank a lot, and Bob kept going on and on about those worms. I still couldn't understand how the floor could possibly have been covered in worms, but I kept that to myself. He was too fucked-up to try and talk any sense to.

Then he started talking about *his* worm, and that was worse. Much fucking worse.

"It won't die, Peacock," he kept telling me. "I'm like a slave to it." And he kept asking me why the doctors wouldn't operate on it, and pulling at his shirt. All I could think of was to ask him how he'd got it.

"Oh, that's a funny story," he said. "That's a funny fucking story."

But he wasn't smiling.

"I had this job once," he said. "It was a fucking low time, and I had this job dressing up as a bunny at a fairground."

"A *what?*"

"A bunny. A fucking rabbit. Handing out these fucking leaflets, in this filthy fucking fairground. And there were these feet with the costume that wouldn't go over my shoes, so I had to do it in bare feet. And the bottom of these bunny feet were open, and the ground was all fucking wet and disgusting. That's when I got it. Fucking funny, eh?"

Like I said, it wasn't the best of nights, and the wee man drank far too much.

In the end he started to panic and shake, and he was saying to me, "Help me get it out, Peacock. Help me get it out."

Sort of weeping.

And then he passed out and fell asleep.

It was a fucking relief by then, to be honest. And I drank on till they closed the bar, half thinking about going back out to that house, to see what the score really was with the floor. I thought if I did that I could maybe finish off the job we'd started too. But the more I drank the less I could remember exactly where the house was, and I finally started thinking of how things would be if I got out there and found out it was just a normal floor.

So when they closed the bar I just helped the wee man up the stairs and dropped him down on his bed.

He came round for a few seconds and asked me how I was.

"I'm fine, son," I told him. "How are you?"

"Exhausted," he said. "I'm fucking exhausted, Peacock."

Then he was gone again, and I went back to my own room

where Bev was still sound asleep - and probably dreaming her Hollywood dreams.

★

"Peacock?"

"Spot-on, pal," I said.

"Peacock? What fucking time is it?"

"You tell me."

I'd woken up early, and I was down in the hotel lobby, phoning my guy back at home, the guy who'd sent me over to hook up with Bob in the first place.

I could hear him scrambling about on the other end of the line.

"It's three o'clock in the morning, Peacock," he said at last. "Where the fuck are you?"

"I'm in LA," I told him. "I'm in LA still trying to get this fucking record made. You and me are going to have to have a serious talk when I get back there, son."

"Aww, come on, Peacock," he said. "You're not still angry are you? You're in LA for Christ's sake. How much better could it have turned out?"

"Listen," I said to him. "Listen. Somehow we've just about managed to get this thing made, no thanks to you and your fucking "contacts". But I need some more money to get it finished, and you're going to send it to me, to help make up for the money I've had to spend because of you, you fucking clown."

He was silent for a while, and then he asked me how much I needed.

"Two grand," I said, and he was silent again.

"You weren't serious about cutting me out of the deal, were you?" he asked, and I took my turn to be silent.

"I'll tell you what," he said. "I'll send you the money, Peacock, by way of an apology. I feel bad about what's happened. But here's the condition. Two grand's a lot of money to pay out, so in return I want twenty per cent of what you make from the record, instead of ten."

I stayed silent again. He fucking had me. There was no other way out of it.

"Alright," I said in the end. "Just as long as you wire me the money as soon as it's morning there."

"I'll send it first thing, Peacock," he said. "The moment I get a fax from you, entitling me to my twenty per cent – with your signature on it somewhere."

"*What?*"

"I've got to cover myself, Peacock."

"Jesus..." I said. "Alright, alright. I'll send it."

I wrote down the number of his machine, and hung up.

What a fucking joker.

X

But the cunt was as good as his word, which came as a fucking surprise to me. The money arrived that afternoon, and we were back in business again.

I'd told Bob the money was coming, just after I'd written that fax, and we'd sent Bev off on another one of her tours while we waited around for it to arrive. It got pretty fucking boring though, just hanging about, so to pass the time we gathered up the money we had left and went out to renew the lease on the car.

Bob seemed alright again. He had a fuck of a hangover on him, but he didn't say anything more about any worms, and I was happy about that.

And he was happy I'd managed to sort out the money, or as happy as you can be with that kind of hangover banging away.

"How did you get him to send it over?" he asked me, as we drove out there.

"He knows he owes me big time now," I told him. "He knows he fucked this thing up right from the word go."

"I'll bet that's all down to my guy," Bob said. "He probably stuck it to your guy just to get at me."

101

"I'm not going to let him know that though, son," I told him. "I'm going to play this fucking thing for everything I can get."

Bob laughed.

"Imagine my guy when this record takes off," he said. "Imagine him when he realises he's catapulted me to stardom. That's going to be fucking priceless."

And he started cracking up.

It was a long way out to that hire place. A couple of times I thought we must have left LA, we'd gone so far. I hadn't realised till then how fucking enormous the place was. But it was well worth the trip.

When we finally got out there Bob showed the guy the lease agreement, and the guy looked at it.

"This expires tomorrow," he said.

"I know that," Bob told him. "That's why we're here. We want to extend it."

"But it expires tomorrow, sir," the guy said. "We can't extend this today. We can't renew the contract until it expires."

"You're fucking kidding me," Bob shouted. "So we have to come back out here again tomorrow?"

"Normally you would, sir," the guy told him. "But in this instance, tomorrow is a Sunday. We're closed on Sundays, sir."

"I'm sorry? You won't let us renew it today because it doesn't expire till tomorrow, but we can't renew it tomorrow because you're closed?"

"Normally you would renew it tomorrow, sir. But in this instance we're closed tomorrow."

"So why did they give me an expiry date that's a Sunday? How could I take the car back or renew it?"

"I guess the place you hired it from must be open on a Sunday, sir. We're not. We're closed."

"Give us a break, pal," I said. "Just fucking renew the thing."

"Excuse me, sir?"

"We're trying to give *you* money, pal. What's your fucking problem?"

"I'm sorry?"

"So what do we do?" Bob asked him.

"I'm afraid you'll have to come back on Monday."

"But we won't be here on Monday."

"Do you know where you will be, sir?"

"We'll be travelling."

The guy started hitting some buttons on a keyboard.

"If you have an idea of where you'll be, sir, I can look on our computer and find you details of the nearest office."

"We'll find it ourselves," Bob said. "Don't worry about it."

"Okay, sir. I'm sorry we couldn't be of more help."

"Fucking jackass," Bob muttered as we left.

Like I said, it was well worth the fucking trip.

But at least it passed the time, and when we got back the money had arrived. We'd won a fucking watch too, cause the cunt had thought I'd meant two thousand *pounds*, not dollars. So there was a lot more than I'd been expecting, and as soon as we'd counted it up we went straight off to see our guy.

He was waiting for us too. He was waiting there and ready to go. In fact, he was a bit *too* ready as far as I was concerned. The cunt had already drawn up a contract entitling him to his ten per cent, and he wanted us to sign it as soon as we got there.

"Hold on a wee minute, pal," I told him, and Bob translated. "Wait till the fucking song's finished. Wait till we see if we like what we're getting first."

But I had to give him his due – once he got going he did a cracking job on it, and he worked fucking quickly too. It was nothing like that night we'd spent in the other recording studio. He just loaded all the individual tracks we'd brought him into his computer, and he mixed them together without any drums. Then he started adding all these banging beats and dance noises. It was all over in no time.

"What do you think, guys?" he asked us, after he'd been fiddling around with one particular bit for a while. "Does that sound okay to you?"

But it had already been sounding perfect to us for ages.

"It's not too far from what we knocked together ourselves in Chicago, eh Peacock?" Bob said, and he laughed.

"You're right, wee man," I told him. "This one's just a bit more... what's the word...?"

"Polished," Bob said, and he laughed again.

But I told the guy that we fucking loved it, and I think he even understood me for once. So we signed his fucking contract and gave him his money.

"You guys get this to DC as soon as you can," he said, and he gave us the details of the place. "I really do think this is going to fly."

"I don't suppose Glen'll be too pleased about it," I said, and Bob translated again.

"I guess not, but fuck him. He's already made his millions. If he was starting up now he'd probably be sampling someone too."

"Maybe," I said. "Maybe."

And then we were out of there. Three fucking hours from start to finish.

"That's the way to really make the money," I said to Bob, but he wouldn't go for that.

"It's nothing compared to what's coming our way," he told me. "Nothing at all."

PART III

I

We left LA early the next morning and Bev was absolutely gutted. It was a terrible thing to have to see. It was terrible because she didn't make any fuss, she just wept and wept.

When she'd got back from her tour I'd let her hear the finished song, just to break her in gently before I told her we'd be leaving. And to try and shut her up about the tour for five minutes too, if I'm being honest. It was starting to drive me mad again.

"There you go, hen," I said, and gave her the headphones. I could hear it tinkling away while she listened to it, and she started bopping about and laughing.

"This is fucking mental, Peacock," she shouted.

"You don't have to shout, hen," I told her.

"What?"

"You don't have to shout."

She pulled the headphones away from her ears.

"I can't hear you," she said.

"I know. But I can hear you. You don't have to shout."

"Oh."

She let the headphones fall back into place, then she started laughing again.

"It's mental, Peacock," she shouted, louder than before. "Totally mental."

It was fucking hard to tell her after that, seeing her dancing about and knowing how happy she still was from her tour. But it had to be done.

We'd had to think up a plan too, me and the wee man, to make sure she'd want to come to Washington with us, rather than staying on there and flying back herself. We didn't have the money to get her a flight and hotels, and take us both across the country, but I couldn't let her know that. So Bob had said to tell her we'd stop off in Memphis and visit Gracelands on the way over. I must admit, that got me pretty fucking excited myself, and that's where I told her we were headed to now, rather than just saying we were leaving LA.

But she still didn't take it too well. She just fell silent and sat down on the bed.

"Don't you want to visit Gracelands?" I asked her, and she nodded quietly. Then she sniffed.

"It'll be fucking magic," I told her, but there was no cheering her up.

Not all night long.

When I woke up in the morning she was already awake and weeping. Just quietly.

"What's up, hen?" I asked her.

"I'm just being daft, Peacock," she said. "I'm just sad."

And she didn't stop. We went down for breakfast with Bob and she sniffed all through it, covering her face up with a tissue every now and again when her sobbing got the better of her, and I watched her shoulders moving back and forwards.

"You'll enjoy the trip when we get going," Bob told her. "This really is the best way to see the country."

She took the tissue away and rubbed her eyes.

"I'll be alright," she said, and she was going to say something else too, but she couldn't get it out.

I'm a fucking fool to myself sometimes, but it was breaking my fucking heart to watch her like that. So on the way back up in the lift I gave her a wee cuddle and told her me and Bob had one more treat planned for her before we left. I told her we were going to take her up to Beverly Hills, as soon as we'd packed, and I told her all about the maps you could get of the houses up there.

It wasn't an ideal move from me and Bob's point of view, but she got pretty fucking excited about it.

"Oh, Peacock," she said. "That sounds wonderful."

And she sniffed hard and wiped both her eyes dry.

While we were up there packing she couldn't stop talking about it, asking me whose houses I thought we'd see, and if we'd see anyone out in their gardens. And we had everything stuffed into the suitcases in no time at all.

I tried to imagine how packing would have been otherwise, if we hadn't been going up there. She'd have picked all her crap up one thing at a time, and dragged herself around the room in tears, curling up on the bed every now and again to cry properly. It all seemed like an okay trade when I thought of it like that.

And you should have seen her face while we stood out on the pavement waiting for the valet guy to bring the car round. She looked like a wean, with her eyes all red and damp, and stuff dripping down out of her nose. The sun was shining on her, and to tell you the truth she looked fucking lovely; all laughing and excited. I wish now that I'd taken a picture of her.

I let her sit up in the front beside Bob when the car came round, and when we got into Beverly Hills she sat with her map spread out in front of her, and she kept turning round to me to tell me whose house was coming next.

She directed Bob to the ones she wanted to see the most, and made him stop at the entrance to each one. Even in daylight there wasn't a lot you could see, past all the security gates and fences and trees. But at some you could see a tiny patch of garden or an area of the house, and she sat staring in the hope that she'd see someone.

"Can you imagine living in a place like that?" she asked Bob at one of the houses. "It would be like you'd died and gone to heaven. You could have ended up in one of those, you know, if you'd gone through with my plan." Then she laughed.

"Oh, God," she said. "Listen, I've just remembered a dream I had last night. I had this dream that we were all walking down Hollywood Boulevard, all three of us, and you were following this girl, Bob. You were walking really closely behind her, staring at her. And then you turned round to us and said, 'She is just *so* Tom Cruise.'"

"I said what?"

"She is just *so* Tom Cruise."

"What the fuck does that mean?"

"Well, I asked you that. In the dream. I said, 'Bob, what do you mean?' And you said, 'That's what I say when someone's sexy. I say they're *Tom Cruise.*'"

That cracked the wee man up.

"Tom Cruise," he said, and he could hardly contain himself. "I like that. Maybe we should tell him if we see him up here."

But we didn't see him. And we didn't see anyone else.

When Bev had sat outside all the houses she wanted to see she had Bob take a quick drive around the whole place again, just to get one last look at it, but she'd already gone back to being quiet by then. She only had him stop once more, and that was when we were almost back at the bottom of the hill, and she wanted to swap me the back seat for the front.

I was in for a surprise when we got outside the car though. She gave me a wee kiss on the cheek, and thanked me for bringing her up there. Then when we got back inside she lay down and we started the long drive out of LA.

And each time we ground to a halt in traffic, and the CD got quieter as the engine slowed down, we could hear the sound of her weeping in there.

II

The simplest route would have been Highway 40, all the way to Memphis. But I looked at the map and saw we could pass through Phoenix on the way.

"It adds a hundred miles to the journey," Bob said. "Maybe more."

But I managed to convince him. I didn't want to miss out on the chance to see the subject of one of Glen's best songs. So we got on Highway 10 and I dug out the Glen CD again and stuck it on.

I played 'By the Time I Get to Phoenix,' on repeat a couple of times, just to get us in the mood, then I knocked it back to the start and let the whole CD play through.

Bev had fallen asleep by then. Her weeping had been replaced by snoring, and she slept on through most of the day.

It was fucking strange to be back out travelling again. I'd almost forgotten what it was like. I'd forgotten how boring it could be, and how much energy it took just to fucking sit there all day without losing your mind.

It was early evening by the time we started seeing signs saying that Phoenix was close, and we hadn't seen much of anything else between there and leaving LA. It had fucking ground me down. But I slowly came back to life when the signs started to appear, and I got the CD back on again, and rubbed my hands together to wake myself up properly.

It wasn't long before Bev's head appeared between the two front seats then either. She struggled to get her eyes open and peered out through the windscreen.

"Where are we?" she asked, looking confused.

"Near Phoenix," I said.

She squinted and screwed up her face.

"What's that?" she asked.

"Where?"

"Up there. Is that a teapot?"

"Aye."

"Who's is it?"

"Bob's. He bought it in LA.

"I thought it looked pretty Tom Cruise," Bob said, and she laughed.

Then her head disappeared again.

The buildings started to appear on both sides of the road, and soon we were on the main road running into town. The sun was getting low, and I had to play the song once more. It felt fucking magic to be almost there. We kept travelling down this road and there were hotels and fast food places and petrol stations on both sides, and it felt fucking mental to almost be at the place the song was about. Every time I'd ever listened to it, it had brought a vague picture into my mind, and now I was about to see what it was really like.

We climbed up on a road that swept off to the right, amongst all these other roads bridged over one another and sweeping off in all directions.

"Fuck..." Bob said. "Where the fuck am I going?"

"Just head for the centre of the place," I told him.

"Fuck," he said again, and he tried to cross the flow of traffic to get us over onto another road.

He swung across and then swung across again, and I caught the teapot as it slipped towards me.

"You know what, Peacock," he said. "I think that was it."

"That was what?"

"Phoenix. I think that was it."

"What was?"

"That road we came down to get here. We were on our way back out again there."

He'd got us back onto the road we'd come down, and we were on the other side of it now – going back up.

"It can't be," I said. "We must have missed a turning."

Bev reappeared between the seats again.

"I'm starving," she said.

"Me too," Bob replied. "Will I stop somewhere up here?"

"Hang on a minute," I told him. "Let's just find the fucking place first. Let's find the centre of town and we can get something there."

"This is it, Peacock," Bob said. "This is all there is."

I couldn't fucking believe it.

Bob struggled to find a way off the road we were on, to get us to the food places down the side of it, and we ended up on a rickety road behind them all, driving down there till they found somewhere they fancied.

When they went inside I had to stay in the car for a few minutes on my own, trying to get a fucking grip on it. I just couldn't believe it. It didn't make any sense. And I just sat there watching the sky getting dark, and feeling totally fucking shattered.

★

We got out of there as quickly as possible after we'd eaten. I'd half thought - earlier in the day - that we might end up getting a room there for the night, but we got to fuck as soon as we could.

We drove back onto the road that swept up to the right and soon there was nothing but scattered houses again, like we'd seen on the way in before we hit that strip road, and there was no particular pattern or sense to where the houses were. They were all just scattered across the place at random.

"What a fucking town," I muttered.

"It looks like someone just dropped it from the sky," Bev said. "And then let everything lie just wherever it landed."

Glen's CD had started up again when Bob turned on the engine, but Bev leant forward and took it out of the machine.

"I think we need a break from this," she said, and I agreed. We did. But we didn't need what she put on instead. She put on her own fucking CD.

"Aww, come on," I said. "For fuck sake, Bev."

"Leave me alone," she said. "I'm just starting to feel better, and this reminds me of being back in LA."

She played it another twice through after it ended, and it blared on as we headed up towards Highway 40.

"I'll stop at a motel once we get up there," Bob said. "Then we're on a straight run to Memphis in the morning."

"I hope that doesn't fucking let us down like this place did," I said.

"It won't," he told me. "It's Memphis, Peacock. It's not fucking Phoenix."

"Let's hope not," I said, and I wished I'd never talked him into making the detour. We could have been a hundred miles further along by then, and I wasn't sure if the song would ever recover. If it did, it was going to take a long time.

A long fucking time.

III

There were three surprises waiting for us when we left our motel the next morning, groggy and still half asleep. The first one was pretty small, but it started to wake us up all the same. It was the sound of Bev's song coming on, really fucking loudly, as soon as Bob sparked up the engine. We all jumped, and I pulled it out of the machine and threw it into the back.

"Put that away," I told her. It wasn't the sort of song you wanted to start the day with, especially not at that fucking volume.

Our next surprise was how fucking gorgeous the scenery was once we got into New Mexico, especially after the boredom of the day before. And that helped to wake us up too. Bev even made a wee joke when we were crossing over from Arizona.

"Here comes the State-line, Peacock," she said. "Do you want us to stop and let you get in the boot?"

But the third surprise was the one. That was what the other two had been getting us ready for, and it happened not too long after we'd crossed into New Mexico.

We were still amazed at the scenery, pointing things out to each other all the time, and then Bob pointed something out to us. Something back behind us.

"Shit," he said. "That's not good."

Bev and me turned round to see what it was and it was a light.

112

A blue flashing light.

"Fuck it," Bob said, and he slapped a hand on the wheel.

The light got closer and closer, till it was sitting constantly behind us, and Bob pulled over to the side of the road.

They pulled in too, and sat behind us for what seemed like fucking ages with the light still flashing, and Bev kept asking what was going on. We told her we had no fucking idea, and hoped we were right.

"I was on the speed limit," Bob said, and looked up at the teapot.

Slowly, the driver's door behind us opened, and the cop started walking towards our car. Bob rolled his window down, and soon the face, the hat, and the massive fucking sun-glasses were all in there with us.

"Morning, guys," the cop said. "Good morning, ma'am."

"What's the problem, sir?" Bob asked him.

Bob didn't look too good. He looked about as bad as when we were driving away from that house and he'd just had his worms experience. But the cop didn't answer him. I don't think he even looked at him, although it was hard to tell where he was looking with those fucking enormous shades on. It was impossible to tell if he even had any eyes.

He stood there without saying anything for a bit and then he pointed at the teapot.

"You guys brewing up?" he asked, and he told Bob to pass it out to him. He looked all around the outside of it and then lifted the lid.

"Jesus H. Christ," he said, and quickly put the lid back on. "Take this off me," he told Bob. "That is *bad*."

Shakily, Bob took it from him and put it back on the dashboard, and in a quiet voice he asked again what the problem was.

"The problem is," the cop said, "this vehicle was reported as stolen. Step out of the car, please."

By then the other cop had appeared, and in a moment me, Bob and Bev were all standing with our hands on the windows and our feet apart, having guns knocked against the inside of our legs to feel for other guns.

"I think there's been a misunderstanding," I heard Bob say.

"Uh-huh," the cop replied. "Keep your hands on the vehicle, please."

When they were happy we had no guns they put their own guns away and I heard the handcuffs starting to rattle.

"This is a hire car," Bob said quickly. "We're on our way to renew the lease in Albuquerque."

I don't know if that's really what we were doing. To be honest I'd forgotten all about the fucking lease again, but it seemed to slow them down.

"The information I have, is that the lease on this vehicle expired twenty four hours ago," the first cop said. "That means this vehicle is now classified as stolen."

Quickly again, Bob told him the whole sorry story of us trying to renew it, and of the chain being closed on Sundays.

The first cop muttered something to the second one, and the second one muttered something back. They let us turn round then, and the first one went off to their car to use the radio.

"So," the second one said after he'd been gone for a bit, and we were all just standing there wondering what the fuck was going to happen. "So where are you all coming from?"

"From LA, sir," Bob told him. "I'm from New York City, and these guys are from Scotland. I'm showing them the country."

"Scotland?" he said. "That's a beautiful country. What do you guys think of the United States so far?"

It was a fucking weird question to ask at that precise moment in time, and it was fucking difficult to answer in any way that he would want to hear. What the fuck *can* you say about a country where you hire a car, try to pay to hire it again, and end up standing on the edge of the fucking highway with a cop rubbing his gun up and down the inside of your legs; then asking you what you think of his country.

"This State is just beautiful," Bev told him, coming to the

rescue. "The scenery's just breathtaking. I loved LA too. I'm a big fan of all the old films, so I loved seeing Hollywood. I've been having a great time so far."

"That's a wonderful accent," the cop told her, meaning he hadn't understood a single fucking word. "Where are you headed to now?"

"Washington DC, sir," Bob said. "To see some friends. Then back to New York City."

We heard the car door slam, and the first one started his slow walk towards us again. When he reached Bob he asked to see his driving-license and the lease for the car, and Bob went to get them.

"I'll tell you what's going to happen," he said, when he'd stared at them for a while. "I've radioed ahead to the place in Albuquerque. It's in the airport. They're expecting you now, so I want you to go straight there."

He handed Bob's stuff back to him.

"Where are you headed after Albuquerque?" he asked, and the other one told him.

"DC" he said. "These two here are from Scotland."

He nodded slowly and looked at us.

"That would explain the teapot," he said. "Alright. Get going to the airport."

We climbed into the car and they walked off towards theirs. I pulled my seat-belt on and turned round to look at Bev, and I saw the first one coming back towards us again.

"Here we go," I said to Bob, and he rolled the window back down. This time the shades came off. The cunt did have eyes after all.

"One more thing," he said, and pushed his head further in. He pointed at the teapot.

"That," he said. "Get it cleaned out. Otherwise someone's going to catch a disease."

And then he was gone.

IV

There was a lot of whooping and cheering went on when we got back out on the road, and most of it was from the wee man. As soon as it was clear they weren't following us, he took his hands off the wheel and punched them up in the air. Then he started beating the wheel with his fists, and laughing.

"That was fucking frightening," he said. "Jesus Christ, Peacock; I thought we were fucked."

"What's inside that teapot?" Bev asked then. "Pass it back in here and let me have a look."

I handed to her and she lifted the lid.

"Aww..." she groaned. "That's disgusting, Bob. Did they sell it to you like this?"

"Uh-huh."

"Why didn't you ask them to clean it up first?"

"I didn't look inside."

"Aww, Bob," she said. She put the lid back on studied the outside of it, the way the cop had done.

"It's a nice design though," she said. "You should clean it out, Bob. It might be worth something. It looks kind of thirties."

"I'll clean it out," Bob told her, and she handed it back to me.

Things still weren't simple with renewing the lease when we got to Albuquerque. It turned out that the fucking place we'd got the car from in Chicago was an individual franchise, and not an official part of the chain, which caused no end of fucking problems.

To begin with, the guy at the desk told us the only place we could renew the lease was back in Chicago. Then, when we explained to him about everything we'd been through so far, he gave us a ticket each for a free coffee at a stand further into the airport, and told us he'd see what he could do.

We ended up stranded in there for over an hour and a half, and the free coffee tickets were as good as useless. The stand was so busy with other people who were being fucked about by

116

companies in the airport that we couldn't get anywhere fucking near it.

Still, it was more of a town in there than Phoenix had been, and we did some shopping to pass the time. Bob got himself a new pair of cowboy boots, and I got myself a leather stetson. Bev bought all kinds of tourist shite with Albuquerque written on it, and some cleaning stuff for Bob's teapot.

Then we went back to the desk.

Then we went back to the shops.

Then we went back to the desk.

Then we went back to the shops.

Four fucking times in all before the guy was ready for us. And each time we went back to the shops Bev bought more shite again. I thought the whole thing was going to fucking bankrupt us. But finally the guy got it sorted out and he let us pay him.

"I can't give you a renewed lease here," he told us. "But this sheet should cover it. If you keep this old lease, and keep this along with it, that shows your entitlement to drive the car."

He gave them both to Bob and apologised for the inconvenience. He gave us all another free coffee ticket each too, but we still didn't bother to trade them in.

"That fucking stall's got it made," Bob said as we left. "They'll never go out of business as long as they're making their money from other businesses fucking up. I should look into setting something like that up myself."

There was no whooping and cheering when we got back out onto the road this time, though. Everyone was fucking drained. Bev fell asleep in the back, and I put on some Glen then fell asleep myself. There had been too many fucking surprises for one morning.

★

I really hoped over the next couple of days that Memphis wouldn't turn out to be like Phoenix had been. Whenever we played Glen now I had to skip past that song. It was all

117

fucked-up.

When we finally got to Memphis we got there late, and found a motel just on the way in. And we made a few plans for the next day.

"I'll tell you what we should do," Bob said. "We should take a bit of a break and spend a few hours here tomorrow. See Gracelands properly."

"You lazy bastard," I laughed.

"What?"

"You just want a rest from the driving, son."

"It's been a long journey, Peacock."

"He must be knackered," Bev said. "I'm knackered, and I haven't even been doing anything. Let the wee madman rest, Peacock. He must be about ready to drop."

"I'm alright," Bob said. "Driving's easy. The first job I had was driving comic books across the country. That set me up for it."

"You're a fucking liar, son."

"What?"

"That's the third first job you've told me about. I thought you were a party boy."

"I was a party boy."

"You told me that was your first job. And you told me your first job was with the fucking Boston Ballet."

"I did work with the Boston Ballet. And I was a party boy. But those weren't my first jobs. My first job was delivering comic books. When I was eighteen."

Bev was laughing.

"What in the name of Christ is a *party* boy?" she asked him. "Is that like a rent boy? Were you a rent boy, Bob? I always thought you seemed a wee bit funny, wearing that hairnet all the time. Was..."

"I wasn't a fucking prostitute," Bob shouted, and Bev cracked up. She fell back on the bed and pulled her knees up, laughing hysterically.

"You were, weren't you?" she said, struggling to get the words out. "You were. It's all starting to make sense now."

Bob tried to look angry, but he was having difficulty keeping a straight face, cause of the state she was in.

"I wasn't though," he insisted. "I was a party boy."

"Oh, Peacock," Bev said. "Help me, I'm hysterical."

When she'd calmed down Bob explained to her what a party boy really was, according to him anyway.

"And that was your *job*?" she asked.

"That was my job. There was no fucking prostitution involved."

"That's what he thought," I told Bev. "But he couldn't work out why he was the only one there not making any money."

"Oh, stop, Peacock," she said. "Stop. This is bad. I'll be in tears in a minute."

"So that was your first job?" I asked Bob.

"No. You know it wasn't. My first job was driving comic books. When I was eighteen years old. Sometimes I had to drive a twenty hour stretch, so driving's not a problem for me. I just thought we should see this place properly."

"And it won't be like Phoenix?"

"It's not Phoenix, Peacock."

"You're sure we're not right in the middle of it already?"

"I'm fucking sure. We're just on the way in. It's Memphis, Peacock. We're going to Gracelands."

"Alright," I said. "Alright."

V

And this time he wasn't lying. It *was* Memphis; it wasn't Phoenix. It might not have been the same as the picture I'd had in my head, but it had the right kind of feeling, and it was a real fucking town.

On the way in Bev asked if she could sit up in the front, to see things properly, so I let her. But I couldn't fucking believe what she did up there. See what you make of this. She put her own fucking CD into the machine. She thought we were going to listen to Beverly fucking Johnson. Driving into Memphis. I didn't fucking think so.

"What the fuck are you playing at?" I asked her.

"I *like* listening to it," she said.

"Maybe you do," I told her, "but it's hardly fucking *appropriate*, Bev. This is Memphis. You can't listen to shite like that on the way to Gracelands."

"I can listen to whatever I want on the way to Gracelands," she said. "There aren't any rules about it, and this is what I want to listen to."

"Get it fucking *off*," I shouted.

"I'm *listening* to it, Peacock."

I pushed between the front seats and made a grab for the machine, but she grabbed my wrists.

"*Pea*cock," she screamed.

"Put it off, Bev."

"*No*. You're always trying to spoil things for me, you big prick."

I tried to get near enough to hit the eject button, but she forced my hands away and we slammed into Bob.

"Children," he shouted. "Your father's trying to drive here. Don't make me come back there, Peacock."

"Tell her to turn it off, son," I said.

"No he *won't*, Peacock. Just fucking sit back."

I went for it again, and she slammed me into Bob again.

"Now I'm warning you both," he said. "I won't tell you again."

"There," Bev said, dropping my hands. "The fucking song's finished. I missed it. Put whatever the fuck you want on, Peacock, I don't care."

So I told her to put on the Elvis CD, but she was in a wee huff.

"Put it on yourself," she said.

"Put it on, Bob," I said, and Bob fired it up. Then I sat back in the seat and looked out at it all.

Arriving on Elvis Presley Boulevard was incredible. Fucking

incredible. There were motels advertising twenty-four-hour Elvis films in all the rooms, and everything was just Elvis. And to know that the road was leading to the house where he'd lived, that was fucking something.

Further along the boulevard we saw a sign for Gracelands and Bob followed that, and it lead into the car park.

"Here we go, kids," he said, and he looked for a space. There were two fucking aeroplanes in the car park.

As soon as he stopped I leapt out of the car, but Bev was still in her wee huff.

"I'm going to listen to this *now*," she said.

"What?"

"I'm staying in the car till I've heard this."

"Aww, for fuck sake, Bev."

"Leave me to listen to it, Peacock."

"But we're here, Bev."

"Leave me," she said.

So me and Bob wandered about the car park while she listened to her fucking song.

We wandered over to the planes and had a look at them. They both had Elvis' lightning-flash logo on the tail, with the letters 'TCB' above.

"That must have been mental," I said to Bob. "Imagine having your own plane to fly about in."

"It won't be long," he said. "Just wait till this record comes out."

"That would be mad," I said, and we laughed.

We walked back over to the car and we could see Bev's lips moving as she sang along with herself. I banged on the window and she put her finger up and pressed it against the glass. She stuck her tongue out.

"Come on," I shouted.

She shook her head and turned it up louder, and she started singing again.

When it finally finished she came out.

"Is that you happy?" I asked her.

"Fuck off, Peacock," she said. "Get out of my hair."

★

In one of the shops Bob bought a necklace in the shape of Elvis' lightning-flash. It was encrusted with fake diamonds and it had the letters above it where the chain went through.

"What does TCB stand for?" Bev asked him when he showed it to her.

"Taking care of business," he said. "That was his slogan."

"They've certainly put it into practice here," she said. "This place is a fucking joke."

One side of the road was all shops where you could buy all the Elvis stuff you could ever imagine, and a whole lot that you could probably never imagine. And there were cafes and restaurants among the shops too, all selling the different foods that were Elvis' favourites.

On the other side of the road was Gracelands.

"What the fuck are you talking about?" I asked Bev. "How's it a joke? This place is fucking magic."

"It's a rip-off, Peacock," she said. "What does any of this stuff have to do with Elvis?"

"It's got a lot more to do with Elvis than any of that crap in LA had to do with Hollywood."

"Don't talk shite, Peacock."

I pointed across the road.

"There's his fucking *house*, Bev," I said.

"Fair enough. But all the rest of it's shite. And look at the fucking queue to get across to the house. You'd have to stand in that all day, after you'd paid a fortune for the pleasure."

"It won't cost any more than those tours in Hollywood."

"Peacock, stop talking about Hollywood. What's it got to do with Hollywood? Can't I even express an opinion without you jumping down my throat?"

"Not when it's a fucking ridiculous opinion," I told her. "I thought you liked Elvis."

122

"I do like Elvis. Jesus Christ..."

"So what's the fucking problem?"

"Peacock, shut the fuck up. Stop talking to me. You're driving me fucking mental."

We didn't have to queue or pay anything to see the house anyway. You had to pay and queue to get inside, but none of us wanted to go inside. Not least because they herded you across there in a wee spazzy bus, and then dragged you around the house in groups. We crossed the road on our own and leant on the wall, looking over.

"That's fucking something," Bob said, after he'd been standing there silently for a long time. "Just imagine it all happening up there. All the stuff they got up to. Water fights..."

"Water fights?"

"All that," he said, and I stared at him.

The thing that amazed me most was the lack of seclusion. Even just that we could lean on the wall and look over, and from there we could see the house and all the grounds. The house was quite a way in, but the wall was on the main street. It made a change from all those fucking places up in Beverly Hills. It wasn't the sort of place someone with that kind of fame could live in now.

"How about all that?" Bob said to Bev, and she nodded. She was wandering around reading all the messages scratched and written on the wall and the pavement.

"It's incredible," she said.

Some people had left flowers there too, and other kinds of gifts had been pushed into holes in the wall.

We walked further along to the Graceland gates with the musical notes on them. We couldn't get the full effect cause the gates were open, but they were pretty outrageous all the same. And I was amazed again at how low they were.

"I've got to try and go in," Bob said to us then. "I can't resist it. Are we allowed to go in from here?"

"You've got to be on that shitty wee bus," I told him.

"I'm going to try it anyway," he said. "Wish me luck."

There was a gate-man sitting in a booth right at the entrance, and as Bob walked through he nodded at the guy and said,

"Good afternoon, sir."

"Where are you going, buddy?" we heard the gate-man say.

"I'm..." Bob replied, and then, suddenly, he broke into a sprint.

"Hey, *Hey!*" the gate-man shouted, and the door of the little booth flew open.

Bob started running faster then, and he dodged off the main path onto the lawns.

We went back to where we'd been before, to get a better view.

"Hey," the guy shouted again. "Come back here. If you want to come in, you come in on the bus."

Bob turned round to face the guy and dodged about backwards.

"Relax," Bob shouted to him. "Come on, we'll have a water fight. It'll be just like it was."

He started cracking himself up then, doubling up giggling as he dodged about.

"That'll do," the guy said. "You've had your fun. Don't let it go any further."

"Just a little water fight," Bob called back. "Set up the hose. Come over the wall, Peacock. We'll get something going."

Two more uniformed guys appeared at the top of the lawns then, and they started charging towards him. He was only watching the one guy, and soon the other two had him face down on the grass, with an arm pushed up his back. He was still laughing away. He'd given this strange wee shriek when he went down, but he was laughing again now.

"A little bit of wrestling," he shouted to us as they dragged him to his feet, and bundled him towards the gate.

"Alright, guys," he said. "Take it easy now, I'm going."

They pushed him harder for that, and when they reached the gate they pushed him out and he landed on the ground.

One of the idiot buses was just pulling up to the gates when he fell, but he stood up, dusted himself down, and gave them all

124

a wee bow.

"Rough-housing on the king's lawn," he said to us, still giggling away, when the bus had gone inside.

"You're a maniac," Bev told him, but she was laughing too.

"I'll tell you what I'm going to do," he said, and he took his hairnet off. "I'm going to leave this as a gift for the king." And he pushed it into one of the holes in the wall.

The gate-man and the two guards were still standing at the entrance, and he threw a quick glance towards them. Then, all of a sudden, he was back over the wall and standing on the lawn again, whooping.

He watched as they came across the lawn towards him, and then he quickly climbed back to the pavement.

"Let's go," he said to us, and he ran across the road.

"She's right," I told him, when we caught up with him in the car park. "You are a fucking maniac."

He laughed.

"I had to do something, though," he said. "The King would have expected it."

VI

And then it happened again. It happened again, and I couldn't fucking believe it. We were just pulling out of the car park, with the wee man still chuckling away, and the stereo turned itself back on. It turned itself back on at full whack, and Bev's song started belting out of there again.

I nearly had a fucking heart attack, and Bob got such a fright he swerved off to the side.

"For *fuck* sake, Bev," I shouted, and I slammed the thing off.

"What's it got to do with me, Peacock?" she shouted back. "I don't control the machine."

"It's your fucking song, Bev," I told her. "And it's driving everybody fucking mental."

"I can't win, Peacock, can I? I can't fucking win with you."

"What the fuck do you want to win for?"

"I'll tell you what," she said. "You need to learn to manage some of that anger, pal."

"I *what?*"

"You need to learn some anger management."

"What the fuck are you talking about?" I asked her. "What fucking American shite have you been listening to now? I don't need any fucking anger management."

I turned round in my seat.

"*You* need to learn to manage my fucking anger," I told her. "It's got fuck-all to do with me. It's you that makes me fucking angry. Did I get angry before she arrived here, Bob? You drive me fucking daft. You need to learn what makes me angry and then stop fucking doing it. Then my anger *will* be fucking managed."

"You're a fucking belter, Peacock," she said, and that was all.

Anger management.

Jesus *Christ.*

But I did a pretty nasty thing on the way out of Memphis all the same. A cruel thing. She'd pushed me too fucking far, though, and I couldn't fucking help myself. She'd got me all wound up.

I was putting the CD of The King back on - at Bob's fucking request, I might add - and she fucking started again.

"We need some half-decent CDs for this car," she said. "All we ever get is Glen fucking Campbell, and now *him.*"

"Don't forget this fucking shite?" I said, holding up her own CD. "We've hardly stopped listening to this since you fucking made it."

"It's the only thing in here *worth* listening to," she said. "And we'll have to listen to it a whole lot more if we don't get something new."

"Will we fuck," I warned her, and that's when I did the thing. The nasty thing.

I snapped it.

I'll tell you, it wasn't fucking easy either. I bent it one way and it wouldn't give, then I bent it back the other way and it went. A piece of it fucking cut me too, which made me even more mad.

"Fucking *bastard*," I shouted, and I rolled the window down and shoved all the pieces outside.

I was dripping blood onto my trousers, and I wrapped one of the Elvis scarves I'd bought around the cut.

"Look what you've fucking done to me now," I said, turning round to Bev. "Is that you fucking happy now?"

But she didn't say anything. She just looked at me. She looked at me as if I'd smacked her in the mouth – and her eyes started to well up. Then she looked down at her hands, and slowly lay down on the seat, facing in towards the back of it.

"That was too far, Peacock," Bob said quietly. "That was fucking cruel."

"It was hard on me too," I told him, and held up my hand. "Look at the state of that."

There was blood leaking through the scarf, but he shook his head.

"Don't fucking act it," I warned him. "You were as sick of that song as I was." But he wasn't having it.

"That's no excuse," he said, and he shook his head again.

"Ah, fuck off," I muttered.

It was pretty fucking miserable in the car for the rest of the afternoon, after that. No one spoke. I tried to make some conversation with the wee man now and again, but it wasn't happening. It was like that all the way to Nashville, where we stopped to get some food.

"I'm fucking famished," Bob said as we got out of the car, and we started walking along the street to see what was there – but Bev hadn't followed us.

"What the fuck's she playing at?" I said, and I went back and opened her door.

"Are you coming?" I asked her, but she shook her head. She was still lying facing the back of the seat, and I crouched down

127

outside. I put a hand on her shoulder.

"You must be starving," I said, but she only moved her shoulder.

"Get off me, Peacock," she said. No anger, no pleading – just the fucking statement.

"Will we bring you something back?" I asked her.

"My song. Bring me my fucking song back, you wanker."

"Aww, for fuck sake, Bev," I said. "I'm sorry about the fucking song. Okay? You wound me up too much. You were driving me fucking mental. Come on. Come and get something to eat."

"Just leave me, Peacock," she said. "Leave me alone."

I stood up again, but Bob had come over, and eventually he managed to talk her out of there. She gave me this look as she stood up, and then fixed her hair in the reflection on the window.

"You were right," she said to Bob, as we went off looking for somewhere. "I *am* hungry now that I'm standing up."

But she only gave me that look again.

There were plenty of places to choose from. The town seemed to be made up pretty much of one street, but everything on it was either a place to eat or a guitar shop. I pointed out a few places, but I soon got the hint that Bev wouldn't go anywhere she thought I wanted to go, so I left it up to them.

I fell back and took the scarf off my hand to have a look at it. It had stopped bleeding, but the cut was deep. I could pull it apart and have a good old look in there.

That's what I was doing when they suddenly came to a stop. I looked up and realised we were outside a place that we must be going into. They were reading the menu and nodding at each other.

"Will this do?" I asked them, and Bev saw I was studying my wound.

"I wish it had taken your whole fucking hand off," she said.

Fucking charming.

It was an alright place they'd chosen, though. The food was fucking magic, and when it came I realised how fucking hungry I was too.

"I'll tell you this," Bob said, while we ate. "We'd better not let anyone around here know what we're up too. We'd better hope they don't find out what we're about or they'll fucking lynch us."

"How come?" Bev asked him.

"Fucking with their country music," Bob laughed. "They take that shit seriously around here. They wouldn't like it if they knew we'd corrupted one of their songs."

"I wouldn't like it either if someone else had done it," I told him. "It's fucking criminal."

He started smiling to himself, and he laid his cutlery down.

"Maybe we should have some fun with it while we're here," he said. "Maybe we should shake them up a bit." And he started laughing.

So when we'd paid up and got out of there, he got the bag from the boot with the tapes in it, and fished out the CD. Then we drove up and down that street three or four times with the song fucking blasting.

He'd put all the windows down and he kept sticking his head outside as he drove, whooping.

"How about that?" he shouted to passers-by.

The last time we went down the street there were broken lines of people standing along the kerb-sides, watching us going past.

"I think it's time we got going," he said then. "One more trip and they'll be organised enough to come after us."

He turned off the street after that, and started heading out of the town, cackling away to himself.

"It won't sell much here," he said. "I don't care how many million copies it sells elsewhere; it's never going to sell a single copy in Nashville."

It seemed to me he'd have got the same reaction with any song, in any town. If you see some cunt driving up and down the road with the stereo pumping full-blast, hanging out the window whooping and shouting, sooner or later you'll stop and look. And not long after that you'll try and fucking kill them. Still, he was happy. And it kept him happy driving long into the night; out of Tennessee and into Virginia.

"It sounded good though, eh?" he said to me when we were a long way out of there.

"It sounded fucking magic, son," I told him.

"It's got a real fucking thump," he said. "It's really going to do something. I'm getting fucking excited now, Peacock. We'll be there tomorrow. We should phone the guy in the morning and let him know we're close. Make sure he'll be around."

"I'll give him a shout," I said. "We've come a long fucking way."

"A long way, Peacock. A lot of stories. But this is just the beginning."

"Let's hope so, wee man," I said.

We stopped some time after midnight. Luckily, the room me and Bev ended up in had two beds in it. Otherwise there would have been a lot of kicking and scratching going on.

I went and sat on her bed before I put the light out, and asked her how she was doing. She hadn't said a single word since we'd got into the room.

"I shouldn't have done that to your CD," I told her. "You just have to learn not to wind me up so much."

She fluffed up her pillows and put her head down on them.

"You're a fucking cunt, Peacock," she said.

VII

First thing in the morning I phoned the Washington guy. It took fucking ages to get through all his different secretaries and minions, but I took that as a good sign. It meant he really had something going on there. It meant it was a proper company, and not just some one-man show.

Finally I got connected to his own phone.

"John Williams?" he said. I liked the way he said it. As if he wanted you to think he thought he was just a guy - like any other - while at the same time you could tell he knew you'd be thinking,

"Fuck *me*; it's *him*."

"Alright, pal?" I said. It didn't make any difference to me; I'd never heard of the cunt before our guy gave us his name.

"How are you doing?" I asked him.

"I'm cool," he said. "Who's speaking?"

"This is Peacock, son. Peacock Johnson."

"Peacock!" he said. "How are *you*?"

The cunt was fucking delighted.

"Aye. I'm... cool too, John. We're almost there, pal. We should be in Washington this afternoon."

"Awesome. That's great to hear, Peacock. I'm excited to meet you guys. And I can't wait to hear this song. From what I've been told it sounds like this could really go."

"It will, John," I told him. "It's a belter, son."

"How has the trip been, Peacock? You've made good time."

"Aye, the wee man can drive. We stopped in Memphis yesterday; went to Gracelands."

"Awesome. I'm jealous, Peacock. You know, I've never been. I'll get there one day."

"You should, John. It's fucking mental. Listen, pal," I said. "I'd better go just now, but we'll see you in a few hours."

"I'll be looking forward to it, Peacock. Have you got directions?"

"We've got the address," I told him.

"Cool. Any problems, give me a call. Otherwise I'll see you soon."

"Cheers, pal. Cheers," I said, and hung up. Then I went to tell Bob it looked good.

I didn't realise till I came off the phone that he'd understood everything I said. No - "What?" No - "I'm sorry?" I took that as another good sign. It made a fucking difference anyway.

"How did it go?" Bob asked.

"Magic," I told him. "He's fucking wetting himself, son. He's convinced it'll be a hit already."

"Of course he is," Bob said. "And wait till he fucking hears it. He'll be jumping up and down."

"Are we ready to go?" I asked him.

"I'm just cleaning this out," he said. "I won't be long."

He was washing the fucking teapot, with the cleaning stuff Bev had bought at the airport.

"I'll go and see how Her Majesty's doing," I told him. "We'll see you outside."

It could have gone either way that morning, with Bev. She was grumpy, but she was talking a bit again, and it could have gone either way. But luck wasn't on my side.

As we drove away the stereo did its trick, and started thumping our own tune. I pulled it out and threw it into the bag with all the tapes.

"It's a different story when it's your song," she said. "You wouldn't smash that up."

"Give it a rest, Bev," I told her.

But the bad luck continued, and that was only a taster for what happened next.

We'd stopped for lunch at a roadside place, and we were drinking coffee, waiting for the food to arrive.

"I'll tell you what I'm starting to miss," she said. "I'm starting to miss a really good cup of tea. I'm getting tired of all this coffee. You just can't get a good cup of tea here."

"You should make one yourself," I told her. "The wee man cleaned out that pot this morning, didn't you, son?"

He nodded.

"I'm still not convinced it's safe, though," he said. "It was foul. They must have been disgusting fuckers in that house. How could anyone live in there?"

I shot him a look, but it was too late.

"In where?" Bev asked him. "I thought you said you bought

it somewhere."

"The..." Bob said, but it was no good. He'd dropped us right fucking in it, and she wouldn't let it go till we'd told her the whole fucking story. There was no way round it, and the only bit we left out was the bit about the worms. We just told her we'd had to get out of there cause we'd been disturbed.

"You fucking *wanker*, Peacock," she shouted. "I don't fucking *believe* you. What the fuck were you playing at?"

"Hang on a minute, Bev," I told her. "I didn't even get inside the fucking house."

"Only because someone came along. If... Oh, fuck. Wait... When we got stopped by the police, you thought that's what it was about, didn't you?"

We kept quiet.

"You stupid fucking *cunt*, Peacock. We could all have gone to *jail*."

"But they stopped us for the lease, Bev."

"*I* could have gone to fucking jail. You're a fucking moron, Peacock. What were you doing breaking into a house anyway, when you've got a fucking record company behind you? It's not as if you needed the money. Is that what you do for fun now?"

She wouldn't let go of that either, so we had to fill her in on all the rest of it. She stared unbelieving all the way through it and then stormed off to the "rest room".

"You fucking *monkey*," I hissed at Bob, when she was gone.

"I'm sorry, Peacock," he said. "I'm sorry. I goofed up."

So it could have gone either way with her that morning, but that's the way it went. And she didn't stay quiet after that either, like she had the day before. She came right out at me. Fucking constant. The journey was a fucking nightmare from there on in.

She started shouting as soon as we got back into the car, and she didn't fucking stop.

"It's all been lies from start to finish," she screamed. "This whole fucking trip. Even before I got here it was lies. I don't know what the fuck's going on anymore, Peacock."

"We've told you what's going on, Bev," I said. "We told you. We just have to get these tapes to DC and then everything will be fine."

"Does Washington have an airport, Bob?" she asked.

"Sure," Bob said. "International Airport."

"Take me straight there," she told him. "Before you go to this record company. If there even is a fucking record company. I don't want to know. I don't want to see the place and I don't want to know anything about it. Just take me straight to the airport."

"Don't be fucking daft, Bev," I told her. "Just calm down."

As it turned out, though, we didn't go straight anywhere. We got fucking lost trying to find the address, and I couldn't concentrate on the map with Bev fucking rattling on the whole time, riling me up. I kept having to stop reading it to snap back at her, and then we'd take another wrong turning and I'd have to try and work out where the fuck we were again. It wasn't fucking easy.

"I'm not kidding, Bob," she started shouting. "Stop following this arse-hole's directions, and take me to the fucking airport."

"I'll take you, Bev," he said, "but we have to find this place first; they'll be closing up soon."

We went round another corner and somehow we were back at the river we'd crossed on the way in. Back there for the third fucking time.

"Christ Almighty," Bev shouted. "Give me the fucking map, Peacock."

She tried to grab it, but I held on. If she'd been reading the map we'd have ended up *in* the fucking river.

"Well, stop and phone the guy," she said. "This is fucking insane."

"You're fucking insane," I told her. "If you'd just give me a bit of peace it'd be no fucking bother. Just shut your fucking hole for five minutes and we'll be there."

"Stop the car, Bob," she shouted then. "Stop the car, I'm getting out. I can't take any more of this."

"We'll find it, Bev," he told her. "It's got to be close."

But she'd gone totally fucking mental. She put her hands over his eyes from the back seat and started screaming.

"Stop," she shouted. "Stop the fucking car, you wee shite."

He tried to pull her hands off, then I tried, but she had some fucking grip on him.

"Alright," Bob said. "I'm stopping. You'll fucking kill us all. Take your hands off me so I can see where the fuck I'm going."

She let go and he pulled in.

"Jesus *Christ*," he said, and he turned around in his seat, but she already had the door open and she was outside.

"Fuck," he said to me.

"Now you see what I'm up against," I told him. "Eh? Now do you see it? She's fucking crazy."

She was out there banging on my window, making a mad fucking gesture at me to roll it down.

I opened the door and got out.

"What?" I asked her.

"Give me the money," she said.

"What money?"

"The money for a taxi to the airport and a flight home."

"Fucking sober up," I told her.

"I'm serious, Peacock," she said. "Give me the money, *now*."

I walked a bit further away from the car and she followed me.

"Take some deep breaths, Bev," I told her.

"What? What the fuck are you talking about, Peacock?"

"You need to calm down, hen," I said. "You've got yourself all worked up about nothing."

"Nothing? What the fuck do you mean? Nothing? You're a fucking corker, Peacock. Just give me the fucking money."

"Calm down," I told her again. "You've got yourself so worked up you're not even thinking straight."

"Peacock, I'm calm. I'm thinking straight. I'll tell you how fucking straight I'm thinking. Here's an example. If you don't give me that money, right this fucking minute, I'm going to go to the police myself, and I'm going to tell them about your wee adventure in LA."

"And what will they charge us with, Bev? Stealing a fucking teapot?"

"You *know* what they'll charge you with, Peacock. And it won't be the fucking first time, either. So give me the money."

"I haven't got it," I told her.

"Don't try that one, pal. Just fucking give me it."

"Bev," I said. "I haven't got it. I'm so fucking sick of you I'd give you enough for a first-class ticket if I had it, just to be fucking shot of you. But I haven't got it. We only had enough to get us here, and now we have to take the tapes to the guy before we can get any more."

She started fucking screaming again.

"*What*? You brought me out here without having any way of getting me *home*? Are you fucking *mental*, Peacock? What the fuck are you trying to do to me?"

She ran back to the car and threw the passenger door open, and I thought she was going to strangle Bob or something. So did he, judging by the look on his face. But in a second she was back out again, slamming the door shut.

"And this is it?" she shouted at me. She was holding up the bag with all the tapes in it.

"Put that down, Bev," I told her.

"This is it? This is my only chance of ever getting home? You've hung my fucking chances on this?"

"Relax, hen," I said. "There's no problem. We'll have all the fucking money we need when we get those tapes to the guy."

"Peacock," she said. "It's a lot of *shite*. This song'll never go anywhere. You won't make a fucking penny from this."

"We will," I told her. "Don't worry about it. The song'll make a fucking mint."

"Will it fuck," she said. "I can fucking guarantee it."

And in an instant she ran across the road.

I couldn't work out what was happening at first. Even when she got to the other side of the road I didn't know. But Bob was way ahead of me. His door flew open, and he started shouting.

He dived across the road in a blur, but he wasn't anywhere near fast enough. The bag was up in the air before he even reached the pavement. And it was only as I watched it crashing down into the river that I caught on.

And the thing sank like a fucking stone.

"*No!*" Bob shouted, and he kept running. I thought he was going to fucking kill her. I thought he was going to push her in. But he ran straight past her and jumped in himself.

I ran across the road then too. He hadn't landed anywhere fucking near where the bag had gone in, but he kept diving under and resurfacing; struggling for breath and then diving back down again.

"Forget it, Bob," I shouted at him. "Get out of there. You'll never fucking find it. They're all fucking ruined anyway."

He gave me a wee wave, and then dived back under again.

But this time he was gone for a long time. Too long a time.

VIII

"You've fucking killed him," I shouted at Bev. "You've fucking killed the wee man."

"Get *in* there," she shouted back at me. "Get in there and fucking find him, Peacock."

"Me? You know I can't swim, Bev."

"Well what then? What the fuck are we going to do?"

"I don't fucking know. What the fuck were you playing at, Bev?"

"I was trying to make you see sense, Peacock."

"Sense? What the fuck are you talking about? Where's the sense? You want to go home and you throw our only way home in the fucking river?"

"Oh God, Peacock," she said. "Do something."

"Do what? What the fuck can I do?"

"I don't know. Do *something*."

But I didn't have to. The wee man came spluttering back up to the surface downstream, and we ran down towards him.

"Bob," I shouted. "Get the fuck out of there. Get out."

He started swimming towards the edge and we went down the embankment. I stretched out an arm and grabbed him.

"You're a fucking nutcase," I told him, and he sat down spluttering on the edge of the water. He was all covered in fucking slime and stuff.

"I couldn't find it, Peacock," he said.

"Of course you couldn't find it," I told him. "You were nowhere fucking near it, son. We thought you'd fucking drowned."

Bev knelt down and put her arms round him.

"We did," she said, but he wouldn't look at her. He tried to shrug her away, then he jumped.

"Fuck," he said.

"What?"

"You've knocked my fucking Elvis necklace off," he said.

It had dropped into the river and he got up onto his knees and started feeling about in the water.

"I'm sorry," Bev said to him.

"You're sorry about that?" I shouted at her. "What the fuck are you on, Bev? What about the fucking tapes? It's only a fucking necklace."

"I've got to get it back, though," Bob said. He was still shivering and shaking from having been in the river. "It's my talisman," he said. "It'd be a bad omen to lose it."

"Bob," I said. "What the fuck are you talking about? The bad thing's already happened. All the bad luck's arrived. We're already fucked, son."

But he wasn't listening. A bit further down the river two weans were kneeling on the riverbank, and they were sharing a face mask, taking shots each of wearing it and looking into the water. Bob had clocked that, and he ran down there.

"Give me that," he shouted at them, and they looked up, fucking terrified, as the wee man stood there soaked and shivering and covered in fucking slime.

"Hurry it up," he said. "Come on, you'll get it back. I need it to find something."

They both stared at him, and the one who was wearing the mask shook his head.

"Give me it," Bob said, and he grabbed at the front of the mask. He started pulling it away from the wean's face, but the rubber strap was keeping it on, just stretching further and further. The wean grabbed the front of the mask too and tried to pull it back the way, but Bob kept flicking his knuckles until finally the mask came off.

"Aah, Fuck..." Bob yelped, as the rubber strap slapped against his hands. But he pulled the mask on and came back up to where the necklace had gone in, with the weans running after him, punching at his legs.

He bent down and looked in, pushing the water around with his hands. And soon he was right in there again – up to his waist – wading about with his face pressed against the surface.

"Bob," I shouted to him. "Give it up, son. You'll never fucking find it."

But he did. Back in close to the edge again. And he came flying up out of the water with the chain dangling from his fingers and he punched his other fist into the air. Bev started fucking clapping. I couldn't fucking believe it.

The wean who'd been wearing the mask ran up to him then and grabbed it back, and the two of them ran away.

"Is it alright?" Bev asked him, as he fiddled about with the necklace.

"The chain's bust," he told her. "But I can fix it. Come on, let's go."

"Go where?" I asked him. "Where the fuck are we going to go?" And that stopped him. No one had any fucking idea where we were going now, and we just sat down there in silence. Staring at the fucking river.

We sat in silence in the car for a while too, still parked up at the

139

side of the road. It was Bob who finally had the first idea for what we should do – as he sat there dripping all over the seat. And it was him who had the second idea too, after the first one had come to fuck-all.

To be fair they were both pretty much the same idea. The second one was just a slightly more desperate version of the first one.

His first idea was to phone our guy back in LA.

"He's bound to have it all backed up on the computer," he said, suddenly becoming all animated. He stopped shivering then, and sparked up the car, and we went off to find somewhere with a phone. But like I said, it came to nothing.

I didn't tell the guy what had happened, I just asked him if he still had a copy of the song, in case we needed it.

"I'm sorry," he said. "We don't keep any of the clients' material. We can back it up for you at the time, if you ask – for an extra charge. But space is limited, so otherwise we clear everything out."

"But you were in on this one," I told him. "You had a cut. We were more than fucking clients."

"I'm sorry," he said.

"You still don't get it, do you, Peacock?" Bev said, when I told them how it had gone. "You still don't understand."

"What?"

"All they wanted was as much money as they could get from you. They always knew it wasn't going anywhere."

"Fuck off, Bev," I told her. "You're still walking a thin line, hen. A very fucking thin line."

Bob's second idea was to phone the studio where we'd recorded the original stuff with the musicians.

"At least if we got that stuff we could rebuild it again," he said, and he went off to phone this time. And he didn't look too unhappy when he came back.

"How did it go?" I asked him.

"He's gone to check," Bob said. "He thought they might have backed it up when they were putting all the tracks onto DAT for us. We've to call back in an hour."

"That's fucking magic," I told him.

"How about we try to find a hotel in the meantime," Bob said. "I need a shower and a change of clothes, Peacock. I'm catching my fucking death here."

So we went off and found a place. The wee man got himself sorted out, and within the hour he was at our door with some good news.

"He found a tape with our name on it," he said. "I told him it was an emergency and he's sending it by courier. It should be here by the morning."

I slapped him on the back.

"We're back on, wee man," I shouted.

So we phoned the guy in Washington and told him the car had broken down. We told him we'd be another day or two and he seemed okay with that.

"Will we be able to find a place here that can remake the thing?" I asked Bob.

"Are you shitting me?" he said, and for some reason then he tried to do an impression of me. A pretty fucking awful impression.

"This is the world capital of techno, pal," he said.

★

I phoned my guy back at home.

"There are a few final bits of polishing we need to do," I told him, and I offered him thirty per cent for enough to finish it. He said he'd take fifty. I managed to get him down to forty-five, and I went off in search of a fax machine to send him another fucking agreement.

"I'll wire you the money the instant it arrives, Peacock," he said.

"Aye, aye - pal," I muttered. "I know how it goes."

And once I'd found the fax machine we all went down to the hotel bar, and we got totally fucking hammered.

EPILOGUE

So we've been back in Glasgow for a couple of weeks now, me and the wife. It took some getting used to at first, after being away for so long. It took a while to get used to being in the same place all the time, stuck in the fucking rain. But it's already starting to feel now like we've never been away.

It doesn't take long, eh?

How about this, though; I had a letter from the wee man this morning. A fucking *letter*.

Eh?

"Dear Peacock..."

Fucking nutcase.

He said he could still feel the hangover from that night in the hotel bar. He said he still felt a bit like he had the morning after that, and a lot of his letter banged on about that morning.

I'll tell you, we were all fucking struggling that morning. We all had fucking belters, and things had seemed pretty grim. But the tape had turned up at the front desk, and the money had turned up too. So we'd phoned round a few studios till we'd found one that could do what we were looking for, and then we drove out there.

The wee man claimed that it was all down to him getting that fucking pendant back. He claimed that was what had put us back in business.

"If I'd lost this," he said, "we'd never be doing this, Peacock.

142

It's brought all the good luck back with it."

All the same, I was holding on pretty fucking tightly to that envelope with the tape in it, just in case Bev decided to go mental again. And when we got to the studio I took the DAT out of it and gave it straight to the guy.

"Spark this up, pal," I told him. "Let's get on with it."

My head was fucking splitting, and I wasn't in the mood for any hanging about. I had this feeling, too, that if we didn't get on with it quickly the whole thing would somehow disappear again. So I got him to fire the tape into the machine and he pumped up the speakers.

And...

Are you ready for this?

It was Bev's fucking song that started blaring out of there.

It was like a fucking nightmare.

I pushed past the guy and hit the fast-forward button, but there was nothing else on the tape all the way to the end. Nothing.

The wee man ran off to be sick, and I asked the guy to show me the way to the phone.

And on the way out of the room, I heard Bev asking the guy if it would be possible for him to put that onto a fucking CD for her.

Needless to say, they had fuck-all else of ours at the studio in LA. That was the full extent of what they had backed up. Her fucking tune.

When we got out of there Bob pulled off his Elvis pendant and threw it as hard as he could out into the street.

"Fucking jackasses," he shouted.

And then there was nothing else left for him to do but drive us out to the airport.

★

So she's not allowed to play that thing when I'm in the house, that's the fucking rule. And I'll tell you, she's been pretty fucking

143

meek since we got back here. She knows how badly she fucked-up.

I know she's glad it was her who ended up with her song back, rather than us who ended up with ours, but she's feeling fucking guilty about it too, and she's been treating me well because of that. In fact, I don't think she's ever treated me this well before. And I'm onto a fucking winner cause, the truth is, I've made my peace with the whole fucking thing. I'm hardly fucking bothered about it anymore. But there's no way in hell I'm going to let her know that. There's no fucking chance. I'm going to ride this thing for all it's fucking worth.

But I might tell the wee man what happened to get me over it, if I ever write him a letter back.

"Dear Evil..."

Fucking hell. Letters.

Jesus Christ.

It was sad to see him go at the airport, all the same. I had a fucking lump in my throat. And Bev was in fucking tears.

I took enough for our tickets from the money that had been wired over and gave him the rest, to get him back to New York.

"It's been a blast, Peacock," he said. "Fuck knows what I'll do when I get back. I've forgotten how to do anything but drive."

He said in his letter he drove for another week after he got back to New York, till the lease on the car was up. Drove up to New Hampshire and fucked about.

You won't believe what he's doing now though. He got a job out in Long Island, painting millionaire's yachts.

How about that?

And that's not even the whole fucking story.

One of the guys he's working with turned out to be a musician, and Bob was talking to him about our wee adventure, and telling him how much he'd envied all the musicians we worked with. He started spouting all that shite he'd spouted to us, about how he wished he could do that sort of thing, but how this fucking worm held him back. And guess what the guy told him.

He said, "Man, music is the best way to get all that evil shit out."

So now the cunt's learning the saxophone. The fucking *saxophone*. Can you believe that?

Fucking mental.

So I might write him a letter back sometime. I fucking hate writing, especially letters, but I want to tell him about this dream I had on the flight home.

It was a fucking corker.

I must have fallen asleep about ten minutes after we took off, and I dreamt we were sitting further down the plane than we really were, maybe in first-class. Bev was on one side of me, nattering away as usual, and even in dreams it was starting to get on my nerves. So I turned round to see who was sitting on the other side of me, and it just happened to be the big man. Glen. In the full fucking outfit: stetson, cowboy shirt, boots – the lot. And it wasn't Glen as he is now either, it was the young Glen.

"I'd like to thank you, Peacock," he said to me, when I turned round. And he shook my hand.

"Thank me for what?" I asked him.

And he said he wanted to thank me for leaving his song as it was.

"That's how it should be," he told me, and then he was gone. I woke up, and that was that.

But ever since then I haven't felt so bad about what happened.

I'm still fucked off about all the money we could have made, but I'm glad now that we didn't ruin the song. I've decided there's already enough of that shite in the world as it is.

And like I say, the wife's treating me like a fucking king now, so as far as I'm concerned I've won a fucking watch.

And at least I didn't end up lying crippled on the bed like my Uncle Tam.

Eh, pal?

Eh?

Ha Ha...

The wee man...

...and the Peacock.

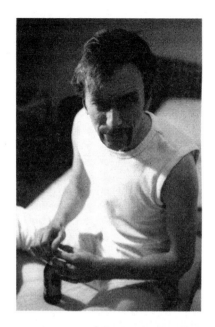

Another hotel...

..another cocktail...

..another hotel...

..another cocktail.

Jackass...

ALSO AVAILABLE ON I.M.P. FICTION

NALDA SAID
by Stuart David

Riddled by an intense fear of his bizarre secret being discovered, the narrator of *Nalda Said* grows up in the strange seclusion of a shoddy caravan with his Aunt Nalda, whose own colourful storytelling leaves him perpetually trapped between fantasy and reality.

Nalda's nephew eventually finds work as a hospital gardener where, perhaps for the first time, he finds true friendship and begins to realise that his dark secret has been suffocating what hope he had of ever leading a normal life.

Finding himself in love, this socially disjointed figure struggles to reconcile his own curious view of the world with the stark daily reality that most people are forced to live with. *Nalda Said* is a compelling and brilliantly crafted tale of one man's pained anxiety and desperate search for his dream - to live a normal life.

"Delicately written and achingly sad, with just a hint of a moral in the poignant denouement, if David ever gives up the day job, pop music's loss could well be literature's gain." *The Times*

"Dark undercurrents of dread and skillful thriller rush... There's an echo of Salinger in *Nalda Said*'s dissection of alienation." *NME*

"Beguiling and ever so slightly unsettling, this is the insular terrain of *The Wasp Factory* and *The Butcher Boy* compassionately revisited." *The Face*

ISBN: 0-9533275-2-3   Paperback, 160 pages   Price: £7.99
Web: www.geometrid.co.uk

THE BAD BOOK
by Stephen Jones

Hit had been happy as an eight year old. He didn't want to grow up. He was a sweet kid, but one that wasn't quite right. He had juvenile insomnia. He was somewhere floating between ME and E-Number hyperactivity. Even the weird bulge under his eye didn't seem to worry him. He was just happy to fall off the edge of the world and get up again. But then his mother goes missing, and all of a sudden he has to be an adult.

This striking debut novel documents a pivotal two days in Hit's bizarre life. It is a desperate, and disturbing tale of one boy's fight to win back a normal life. To find his lost mother and keep tabs on his father, the man he suddenly realises he knows nothing about.

Stephen Jones is the musical blacksheep Babybird. *The Bad Book* is Stephen's first novel, and has nothing to do with music whatsoever.

"Astonishing. *The Bad Book* shares its grotesque childlike detail with Ian Banks' *The Wasp Factory*, but the bleak surreality and contorted memory sequences belong to Jones." *The Times*

"It is breathtaking in its simplicity and its originality. Jones simply has a gift for the sort of words you relish wrapping your tongue around." *The Scotsman*

"Cryptic, yet this cossetted, wounded loner in dystopia will come back to haunt you... 'til infinity." *ID* Magazine

ISBN: 0-9533275-3-1   Paperback, 124 pages   Price: £6.99
Web: www.babybird.co.uk

MILK, SULPHATE AND ALBY STARVATION
by Martin Millar

"What's allergic to milk, collects comics, sells speed, likes The Fall and lives in Brixton? Alby Starvation, the first true British anti-hero of the giro generation. Milk, Sulphate and Alby Starvation is a strange and wonderful story of unbelievable allergies, seedy gutter violence and manic paranoia. I've yet to meet someone who has not enjoyed it." NME

Your doctor refuses to believe you're allergic to just about everything, especially milk, there's a megalomaniac professor digging a hole outside your flat, your small stake in the amphetamine market in Brixton is being threatened by a mysterious Chinese man and the Milk Marketing Board have taken out a contract on your life. Welcome to the bizarre, obsessive world of Alby Starvation.

A world full of shop-lifting, death-threats, paranoia and video game arcades. Alby's frantic struggle to avoid being shot provides the hilarious and engaging back-drop for this, Martin Millar's debut novel.

"A welcome re-issue. This entertaining fable, which is alternately surreal and grubbily realistic, still delights." *The Times*

"Pop cultural references are everywhere in this frantic cultish debut which takes an Irvine Welsh-esque turn." *The Guardian*

"A masterful work that goes straight to the heart of a spurned generation. A work of rare genius and truly cult, it deserves a place on your book shelf next to Hubert Selby Jr's *Last Exit To Brooklyn*." *The List*

"A minor classic... strange, quirky and entertaining to the end."
What's On London

ISBN: 0-9533275-4-X Paperback, 160 pages   Price £6.99
Web: www.martinmillar.com

THE TECHNO-PAGAN OCTOPUS MESSIAH
by Ian Winn

Part bizarre quest, part unique travelogue, part insane fiction, *The Techno-Pagan Octopus Messiah* is an extraordinary tale of prophetic dreams and adventurous treks through Egypt, Rajastan and northern India.

Winn disguises himself as a tourist and, catalysed by drugs from the Amazonian rain forest, takes the reader on a kaleidoscopic trip to places where crystals are dragon eggs, free love is expensive and tourist massacres mean discount hotels. Along the way lies among other things, a tantric commune, an illegal hike up the Pyramid of Chepren, and cryptic encounters with Indian snake saddhus.

Ian Winn is a leading star of the spoken-word circuit. His volatile performances have won high acclaim across both Britain and the USA.

"If you are looking for something a bit different this year, try Ian Winn's debut novel. It has all the travel fiction requisites in spades. Delivered with crazed enthusiasm and humour, it makes a refreshing change from the usual backpackers novels." *The Times*

"Inventive, brilliantly realised characters... displays a rampant thirst for mysticism and self-discovery. One can not help being won over by Winn's enthusiasm and intellectual energy." *The Sunday Times*

"The most progressive, alternative life-style novel of the decade." *Dream Creation*

"One astonishing book!" *Select*

ISBN: 0 9533275 1 5   Paperback, 288 pages   Price: £7.99
Web: www.octopusmessiah.com

LOVE AND PEACE WITH MELODY PARADISE
by Martin Millar

This is the story of Melody Paradise. You'll like her - everybody does. Women aspire to be like her and men fall in love with her. Melody is kind, spiritual and very beautiful. She's also on a mission... and nothing is going to stand in her way.

The travelling community to which she belongs has become horribly fragmented by a series of mysterious and chaotic happenings. Her mission is to reunite them. She organises a festival as the perfect vehicle to bring them together, during which an amazing story unfolds, often funny, sometimes sad, always compelling... and with a twist in the tail.

Through the words and eyes of Martin Millar, the reluctant guest novelist at Melody's festival, we become privileged observers of a world most of us would struggle to even imagine.

Martin Millar - Glaswegian hero to the post-punk generation, low-life socialite, pessimistic optimist, and incurable romantic. Also author of a host of cult classics including *Milk, Sulphate & Alby Starvation*, and *The Good Fairies of New York*.

"Brixton's answer to Kurt Vonnegut." *The Guardian*

"A charming tale... very funny." *Melody Maker*

"Hilarious and endearing comedy." *Scotland on Sunday*

ISBN: 0-9533275-0-7 Paperback, 288 pages   Price £6.99
Web: www.martinmillar.com

HOW TO ORDER:

Visit us at:

www.impbooks.com

for more information on titles, reviews,
author biographies and our music book label,
Independent Music Press, home to titles on
Stereophonics, Travis, Prodigy, David Bowie,
Beastie Boys, Shaun Ryder and more.

For any queries or for a free catalogue,
e-mail us at: info@impbooks.com

TO PURCHASE BY POST

Please make cheques/postal orders or
international money orders payable in £Sterling to:
I.M.P. FICTION LTD
and send your payment to:

I. M. P. FICTION (PJ)
P.O. BOX 14691,
LONDON SE1 2ZA

Please allow 21 days for delivery.
Postage and packing is FREE in the UK,
£1 for Europe and £2 for the Rest of the World.